Peril in Pittman

by

Mary Ann Jacobs

*The Berkshire Mystery Series, Book
Two*

Dedication

I would like to dedicate this book to my patient husband who gave me space to write without interruption. I understand how difficult this was. I also would like to dedicate this book to my Massachusetts family who exposed me, a city girl, to the many festivals and the wealth of theater and the arts in the Berkshires.

Acknowledgements

I would like to thank my editors: Karen Martin, Paula Wolfe, and Imogene Ensweiler for doing a page-by-page edit of my book. They kept me on track and pointed out any inconsistencies. I would also like to thank the members of my Writing Workshop and the Kenton County Writers' Club for giving me honest suggestions to improve so many chapters. Also, a thank you goes out to Cindy Tretter for helping me choose the title, and to the many readers of *Don't Mess with Me*, book #1 in the Berkshire Mystery Series who kept asking me when book 2 would be out because they needed to find out what happened to the characters.

Chapter 1

Freak Out

BANG, BANG, BANG! I heard a horrible clatter that sounded like a practice gone wrong by a drummer from a local band. The accompanying howling sounded like a wounded dog. When I ran into the alley behind Aunt Florence's restaurant, I was nearly pummeled by soup cans hurled into trash cans by petite Sadie with her long black hair flying in the wind.

Sadie, a Lebanese immigrant and my best friend, was venting in the alley behind Sweet Indulgences. If she didn't vent, she'd fall apart.

"Sadie, what are you doing? What's wrong?"

"Oh, Robin," Sadie wailed. She ran to me and fell into my arms. "I can't stop shaking," she sobbed.

Sadie often threw cans or balls into the trash cans in the alley to calm down and release any tension. She would keep score, and usually by the time she racked up one hundred baskets, she was calm and ready to face any crisis, but I had never seen her like this.

I hugged her tightly and stroked her raven hair. "It's okay, Sadie. It's okay. Whatever is wrong, we can work it out together."

Just as Sadie's shaking began to subside, Sheriff "Johnny-Come-Lately" Houtman burst into the alley. "Sadie, are you hurt? What happened? Robin, a tourist reported hearing noises that sounded like gunshots. What happened?" Sheriff Mark Houtman, who has a crush on Sadie, was determined to protect her no matter what anyone in our small town of Pittman thought of her. Two people had died on his watch, and he was determined to never allow that to happen again. No one will harm his Lebanese dynamo.

Seeing Mark so concerned, Sadie took several deep breaths and tried to pull herself together. She managed to choke out, "Omar Habbib, from my village in Lebanon, moved here and has been living in Great Barrington. He came into Sweet Indulgences with his little boy, Ahmram, who reminded me of my younger brother, Joseph, when he was little.

"I had quite a crush on Omar Habbib when I was a teenager. He was so kind and his looks? Wow! He was so tall and handsome, with his dark hair and flashing eyes. We called him H to distinguish him from his father, Max, who owned the corner grocery store. H and I reminisced a bit about home and our mutual friends and acquaintances. We laughed at the trouble that he and Alex used to get into."

"Sadie, what do you know about this Omar Habbib? Is there any way he could pose a danger to you?" asked Mark.

"Oh no, Omar was my brother Alex's best friend. They got into all kinds of mischief with their silly pranks in the neighborhood. Alex and Omar helped out Omar's dad on weekends. One time, Omar asked his dad if he could have groceries as pay instead of his usual wages. Then Omar Habbib and Alex delivered the groceries to the old grandmother, Frieda, who was ill and frail. That isn't the type of person who would be a threat to me."

Sadie told us more about Omar Habbib's situation. "I asked him, 'Why didn't you ever contact me to let me know you were okay?' He proceeded to tell me how, when his family had safely made it to Jordan, he met a girl, Marnie, and fell in love. They were brave enough to get married in those troubled times, and she immediately got pregnant with Ahmram.

"When I last saw Omar and Alex, they had gone into hiding because they found out the ISIS soldiers were coming to our village to recruit and capture young men for their cause. I miss Alex so much. I've often wondered if he somehow is still alive, but if he were alive, why wouldn't he find me and contact me?"

"Whatever happened to Omar's wife?" asked Sheriff Houtman.

"I asked Omar what happened to his wife," Sadie said. "Because of all the trauma she had endured during her flight from Lebanon, he said she was physically very weak, and pregnancy took away more of her physical stamina. Four weeks after Ahmram's birth, she died. Omar was heartbroken and struggled to hold himself together to raise Ahmram. Thankfully, his parents had followed him to the refugee camp and were there to help him. They stayed in the camp and raised Ahmram while Habbib went off to fight with the Resistance Fighters in Lebanon.

"Omar Habbib returned to the camp three years later, exhausted and determined to take Ahmram to safety. Grateful that his parents had taken good care of his son, he offered to take them along on his journey to safety in America. They weren't ready to start a new life in a new world but just wanted to go back to their old life in Lebanon.

"Ahmram left with his dad to go to Great Barrington, Massachusetts, in the Berkshire mountains. Omar's brother, Samuel, was a lawyer there and had drawn up all the necessary legal documents to get Habbib approved for refugee status. Omar's separation from his parents was wrenching, but necessary for Ahmram's future."

Sheriff Houtman was sympathetic, but a bit jealous that Sadie's former boyfriend was now in town. "Why did Habbib come here to Pittman?"

"When Omar explained to me why he came to Pittman, he said, 'When my visa was approved to be near my brother, I decided to make my way to the Berkshires. For three years, I could only find part-time work and helped Samuel as a clerk in his office.'

"Recently, he had heard that my Aunt Florence owned a restaurant in Pittman. He remembered how kind she was to him when he was a teenager. She had practically adopted him since he hung out with her nephew, Alex. Omar decided to bring Ahmram to Aunt Florence's restaurant to taste authentic Lebanese cooking. He was surprised to find that I had also come to Pittman. He was so glad to see that I was safe and healthy.

"It's so sad," Sadie told Mark. "Omar Habbib was just like another brother to me when I was young. As I grew older, I cared about him and envisioned our life together as husband and wife. It probably was just a teenage fantasy on my part. As I look back on the situation, I realize that H was interested in me only as a friend and Alex's little sister."

"By the way," said the sheriff, "whatever happened

to Alex?"

"I never found out, and Omar wasn't sure. Alex just disappeared when the insurgents stormed into our village."

Sadie started to shake again as she lamented, "As Omar's six-year-old son, Ahmram, was diving into his chocolate fudge sundae and smearing chocolate all over his grinning face, all I could think about was Alex and my younger brother, Joseph, who would have been Ahmram's age. Where was Alex? Why did Joseph have to die? Why couldn't it be him licking his lips as he savored each bite?"

Mark Houtman, to his credit, kept quiet and held Sadie as she finally regained her composure.

I said, "Sadie, you're part of our family now. You'll always have your memories, and maybe having someone from your hometown will help you deal with the pain of those memories."

"I did promise Omar that I would tell him about my journey someday when the feeling isn't so raw. He was very understanding."

Chapter 2

Video Documentary Series

When I left Sweet Indulgences, I worried about Sadie. At least Billy was still staying at her house. It provided someone for her to mother. It was helpful for Billy also, since he had no family.

As I headed to Bookworms, I thought about all the trauma Sadie and Billy had endured. Yes, I had lost my beloved husband, John, but maybe I was still luckier than some.

The next day, when I arrived for lunch, I confessed to Sadie, "I'm so nervous. Something has come up. I think it's a good thing, but I don't know. Cameron Coldren, this famous newsperson from Boston, is doing a feature on the contrast between big city and small town's way of life, and he chose to feature Pittman in his Video Documentary Series on BPR. He wants to interview me."

"Oh, Robin, I've heard several of his podcasts," said Sadie. "We often put on his radio show on Friday afternoons. Several of my customers are fans. His focus in the podcast is on interesting or quirky people. The last podcast I heard was about a young husband who lived on the block near the starting point of the Boston Marathon. The husband approached the policeman a few days before the marathon began. From what I remember, he said 'Officer, my wife and I have a problem. She's expecting a baby, and her due date is the day of the Boston Marathon.

"'I spoke to the hospital admissions person to see if we could just admit her the night before the marathon begins, but he wasn't open to that idea because it could be days before delivery.' The administrator told him that due dates aren't set in stone, so they can't tie up a room for many days just in case his wife goes into labor. The administrator said to call if she goes into labor before the marathon, and she can be admitted.

"The poor man sounded anxious, asking the officer what to do if his wife went into labor during the marathon. He worried the roads to the hospital from their neighborhood would all be closed.

"Cameron mentioned the officer's kindness. The officer told the man that he would take care of everything. He would be standing on that very corner and would take them right through the traffic and get them straight to the hospital on time."

Sadie continued, "These are the type of human-interest stories Cameron Coldren reported on his podcasts and the type of stories my customers love. In addition to his weekly radio shows, he also has started a series of video documentaries about the New England area. These are on TV once a month and are becoming quite popular. The next series is going to be about small town living in the Berkshires. That must be the one he wants you to interview for."

Sadie and I talked about what small town life means for us. I said, "Summer weekends in this sleepy small town in the Berkshires come alive with farm festivals that include bluegrass music. It reminds me of the music and sites of my hometown in Kentucky. I do miss my home, but Pittman is becoming a new home that I love."

"I love the summer stock theater and the performances at Tanglewood and Shakespeare and Company," Sadie said.

I said, "I really appreciate the Boston Symphony's summer camp for aspiring musicians. What a wonderful opportunity for developing young talent. These are the opportunities unique to our small town and the small towns of the Berkshires. When summer turns to fall, the locals begin to prepare for the coming of the ski season, which often begins as early as mid-November. Cameron should attend these venues and even attend our planning session for the winter sporting events. I hope he will appreciate our welcoming atmosphere that tends to be different from that of large cities."

As Sadie talked about the Video Documentary Series, I was finishing my second chocolate chip cookie, and Lola burst through the door. "Have you heard? Cameron Coldren, that handsome newsman for BPR, is coming to our town on Friday. Do you think I can wrangle an introduction?"

Point #1 for the Video Documentary Series–News travels fast in a small town.

Lola then commanded our attention by striking a dramatic pose and proceeded to act out her anticipated meeting with Mr. Coldren. "I say, Mr. Coldren, you must be a smart man. I listened to all your past video documentary series and was so impressed. I wonder if you would do me the honor of dining with me?" She fanned herself with a huge old-fashioned fan, blinking her eyes flirtatiously.

Lola, our resident actress, then got this dreamy look on her face and continued, "Can you picture it? Cameron and me getting married on the banks of Lake Onata with daisies in my hair, a white flowing dress, and a bouquet of yellow flowers. Mmmmmm! Maybe they will even film it for TV."

"Lola," I said, "you need to get back into the theater and put that talent to better use than emoting over a man you've never met." I turned to Sadie. "Ah, to be that young again."

"Robin, it's certainly not too late for romance. You're only thirty-nine," said Sadie.

I ignored Sadie and asked Lola, "But what about Deputy Murphy? I hear he has a standing order for a bouquet to be delivered weekly to a certain young lady."

Lola blushed.

Sadie teased, "What kind of flowers do you think Mr. Hunk Coldren would choose?"

It felt good to laugh. Sadie seemed to have recovered from her target practice and was getting back to normal after the summer scare with Billy. Romance is in the air with Lola's dreaming, Sheriff Houtman's constant presence at Sweet Indulgences, and Deputy Murphy's sudden interest in flowers. I seem to be the only one not smitten by summer love.

Lola said to us all, "I want to share my exciting news with everyone. I've landed a part in *The Taming of the Shrew* at Shakespeare and Co. I will be Kate, the wild one. We start rehearsals next week. I will need Wednesdays and Thursdays off, if that's possible, Ms. George."

I was stunned. "Of course, you can change your

hours around to accommodate practices. I'm so pleased you're going ahead with your career. I was afraid I was holding you back," I said. "Lola, would you like me to ask Mr. Coldren if he would want to attend your dress rehearsal on Thursday? Then we could go backstage, and he could properly meet the actors."

"Um, darn, that probably isn't a good idea. Deputy Robert Murphy mentioned that he wants to take me out Thursday night for dinner to celebrate my successful return to the stage. What a line. How does he know I'll have a great performance if he hasn't seen it yet, but I did tell him yes, so I need to find another way to meet Cameron."

"Well, I'm off. Going to stop at the bike store and take Billy and Wayne some cupcakes. I haven't seen much of Billy since he moved in with you, Sadie, and became part owner with Wayne of Hot Wheels, the bike repair shop and motorcycle showroom," I said.

"Billy spends all of his time after school and on weekends in the Hot Wheels repair shop, and Wayne meets with customers in the Hot Wheels' showroom. He sells some high-end Harleys to tourists who like having a bike to cruise around the hills and mountains in the Berkshires. I only see Billy for a late supper, then he crashes into bed. He's so tired, but I guess I am lucky he is so engaged. That way, I won't have to worry about him getting into trouble," said Sadie.

****

When I walked into Hot Wheels, I was impressed with the many motorcycles displayed in the showroom. "Hey, Billy," I called out. "I brought you two a treat."

Billy poked his head out from behind a gorgeous Harley with red stripes. "Hi, Ms. George. Thanks a lot.

I haven't had much time to eat. I needed to do some quick repairs on the Harley before it goes out to a customer today. I came straight here from early morning band practice. We had a problem at band and I got out late."

Billy described the problem. "Three of our expensive new instruments are missing: a saxophone, a mellophone, and a top-notch drum set. Everyone is upset. Ms. White asked some pointed questions of each band member. I think she is convinced it's an inside job. Mike is worried because since his dad went to prison, and Mike now lives with you and Asher until he completes his senior year, the sheriff possibly thinks Mike would steal to get spending money. Sheriff Houtman was going to question everyone, but I begged out so I could get to work."

Maybe Billy should have stayed to talk to the Sheriff. Billy doesn't need any more accusations levied against him after being the prime suspect in the murders last summer.

Billy further related, "Ms. White, the band director, praised my expertise yesterday on the mellophone. She said, 'My stance is perfect with head held high, and hands poised on the buttons.' I was proud that she singled me out. I wish I had had a mother like her to praise me as I worked on my music. Ms. White also gave us all a pep talk after Saturday's competition. She called the band members and the parents together for an after-performance review session. She praised me right in front of the parents.

"Ms. White said she appreciated my diligence as I learned our routines and admired my professionalism. The band members burst into applause.

"After the pep talk, Ms. White got serious, saying we have a problem that needs to be brought to everyone's attention. Some of our new instruments are missing. They were very expensive and bought with the money we raised as Band Boosters. She wants our help in locating the instruments. She said she also involved the sheriff who will be questioning us, and to cooperate with him."

"Be sure you let the sheriff know you are available to talk to him whenever he wants," I told Billy. "Don't wait for Sheriff Houtman to approach you, so that he knows you aren't hiding anything."

"Sure, Ms. George, I get it."

Billy went back to work and mulled over Ms. George's advice. About an hour later, Billy got a text from Mike.

—I need to talk to you and Asher tomorrow morning before band practice. Meet me under the bleachers.—

Mike was walking home after being interrogated by Sheriff Houtman and Deputy Murphy. He was fretting about why his dad hadn't yet written to him from jail to check that Mike was doing okay while he stayed at Ms. George's house.

When Mike got home from school, Asher was doing his homework, and Ms. George wasn't home yet, so Mike went and picked up the mail from their mailbox and was surprised to see a letter addressed to him from Colby Prison. He had applied to several colleges for early admission, but Colby Prison certainly wasn't one of them.

Mike hurriedly opened the letter and then sat on the swing on the porch to think.

The next morning, Mike and Asher got to school early to meet with Billy. Billy looked tired, which wasn't surprising since yesterday's schedule demanded that he go to school, go to the store to work for a few hours, then head back to band practice. Thank goodness, Sadie owned a restaurant so Billy could pick up a sandwich for dinner on the go.

Asher, of course, looked cheery as usual. He's the type of person who seldom gets down, and he faces each challenge with enthusiasm. These two make for the perfect balance to Mike's melancholy self. As he approached his friends, Mike thought, *I know people don't see me as a sad person because I mask my feelings by joking around, but I do show my true self to my two best friends.*

Mike's friends looked worried, but so was Mike. He told Asher and Billy, "When the sheriff questioned me about the thefts, I don't think he believed my reason for staying late in the band room. I think the sheriff thinks I stole the instruments to sell for spending money. How could I have gotten the instruments home and then sold them? Did he ever think of this? When I protested that suspecting me was ridiculous, he just stared at me and said, 'Be careful what you say, Mike. I'm not as trusting as Robin and Sadie.' I'm sure the sheriff doesn't trust me."

Mike then told the boys about the letter he got from his dad. "This is the first letter he has written to me since he went to jail for aiding the kidnappers. The gist is that he's sorry for everything. He's found a self-help group that meets weekly, and he promises me he's turning his life around and is sorry for abusing me over the years. I'll believe it when I see some evidence.

"Listen to this part of the letter:

"'Mr. Omar Habbib, Sadie's friend, contacted me with a proposal for my Ten Pins Bowling Alley, which is closed until I return. He offered to reopen and run the business until I get out of prison in five years or sooner if I'm granted parole. Mr. Habbib proposed a limited partnership. He will take a large percentage of the profits he makes to support himself and another part-time employee. The rest will go to rent and supplies.'

"'This agreement will be in effect until I am released or until you graduate if you decide you want the business. What do you think?'"

"Is it true this is the first letter he has written you? He doesn't even ask you how you're doing. He sure isn't my idea of a supportive dad. Listen, don't make a hasty decision," said Asher. "Let's discuss this with my mom and Sadie tomorrow at Sadie's barbeque, okay? I trust the two of them to give you sound advice."

"Good idea. Sadie will know if Mr. Habbib is reliable since she has a history with him from Lebanon," suggested Billy. "We also need to tell Sadie and Ms. George that the sheriff seems to be determined to accuse you, Mike, or me of stealing."

Chapter 3

More Thefts at the Closing Weekend of the Adventure Park at Jiminy Peak

Mike and Asher were both working a shift from ten to nine at Jiminy Peak's Ski Resort that weekend. There was quite a large crowd of townspeople and tourists flocking to the summer adventure park to enjoy the final weekend of the summer season. Jiminy Peak would close next week to revamp the park into its main purpose, ski slopes, a popular destination for skiers all over the northeast. This was the final weekend for the park, and Ms. Caster, the manager, went all out to make it a success. Booths were set up all around the park in hopes of raising a lot of money to support future plans for the park when it reopened for the ski season.

As Asher was selling tickets at the gate, memories of when he was little popped into his thoughts, when his parents brought him to Jiminy Peak to ski in the winter and to enjoy the adventure park when it first opened. The best attraction of all was the giant trampoline, where children were secured in a seat that bounced up and down as high as you wanted, depending on how hard you kicked it.

He remembered his dad watching him bounce and fly up in the air. His dad was much more scared than Asher, who took all the risks. Asher snapped out of his reverie when he saw Mr. Habbib with the same protective look on his face as he watched his son, Ahmram, bounce high up on the trampoline. Asher missed his dad so much even now, after six years. Asher hoped he would never forget his life with his dad before his fatal heart attack.

Asher was busy at the entrance all morning and early afternoon. He took a two-hour break for lunch and roamed around the many booths. Sadie's food tent, of course, had the longest lines, but Marie's bake tent was also very popular. While Sadie was selling her tasty treats, a Middle Eastern-looking young man came by her tent and started asking questions. "Where are you from? What is your family name? Is your family still in your village?" While he was intensely questioning her, she wondered if he was from ISIS hunting her down because of her work in the Resistance.

Sadie had a premonition that it wasn't food the stranger was interested in. *I am going to have the sheriff check into this stranger's background. Something about him seems familiar.*

Mike had set up a booth for Ten Pins, even though the Bowling Alley had not reopened, but if Mr. H. took over for his dad, he would need to readvertise Ten Pins. Mike's Bowling Booth hosted a raffle for a free game and four discount tickets for games. He also posted a sign: Sign up your teams for a bowling tournament.

I set up a booth for the Bookworm Shop with a selection of books for sale that include acting tips, plays, playwrights, and cozy mysteries. I have tickets for a drawing for a new book published this year. Whoever wins, I will tailor the book to their reading preferences.

Horatio Nelson's Pet Shop booth was attracting a crowd because he was demonstrating the joys of owning boa constrictors as pets. Children were begging him to let them pet the boas. Nelson also displayed the fine aquariums one could purchase to hold a boa, and even said, "If you purchase a boa and an aquarium tank, you can get free frozen mice for six months to feed your snake. Step right up, and if you pay now, my assistant, Milo, will settle your snake into the aquarium and take it to your car when you are ready to leave the park." Some parents didn't seem too pleased with their child's interest in having a snake as a pet and suggested he stop pushing the snakes and instead show the kids some of the cute dogs and kittens. Nelson just laughed at them and said, "What's the matter? Are you afraid of a little snake?"

Asher said to Mike, "That man is evil. No wonder Milo is afraid of his dad."

All the booths were a hit with visitors and were doing brisk business.

Saturday night, as she was closing after the hectic weekend, Ms. Caster, Jiminy Peak's Sales Manager, approached Asher and Mike just as they were about to leave. Since both boys were whizzes at math, and she was not, Ms. Caster had hired the teens not only to run a booth but also to keep accurate records of all transactions; she trusted their expertise.

"Boys, we have a perplexing problem, and I'm worried. When I passed out the cash boxes to each game and booth, I carefully counted each box twice. Last week, the carousel till was short about twenty-five dollars. Have you noticed any discrepancies when you entered the data each day? Do you two know anything about any theft, or have you seen anyone sneaking around the booths?"

"No," said Mike. "I counted our till, and it was exactly what it should be. Each weekend night this month, the cash boxes matched the sales unless someone was entering the sales inaccurately. What day was the carousel till short? We'll go back and check. Maybe we missed something."

"I'm very concerned. So far in the past two weeks, I have counted about five hundred dollars missing from the concession and booth's cash boxes, the admission box, and most of the tills from the rides. Whoever took this money knew where the money was kept and how to get into each cash box. I know exactly what is sold and don't just rely on the paper reports from the booth managers. I know that money is missing. Did you notice any suspicious entries on the reports when you came in this morning and reviewed the week's reports?"

"No." Both boys shook their heads and looked as perplexed as Ms. Caster.

"You only rely on what the merchants report to you, so you may have missed it. Let's sit down together tomorrow before we open and go over all sales for the past two weeks, attendance numbers, and the weekend count of fairgoers at each ride. We might have to have you count the money from each till, not just yours.

"I can't imagine any of my amusement park employees breaking my trust and stealing money. Let's verify everything and keep an eye out for any suspicious activity. Especially look for any strangers or town people hanging around the booths or rides who may look suspicious. I'll speak personally to my employees handling any of the money."

"Have you hired any new employees recently?" asked Mike.

"No."

"Today, the only person I saw sneaking around by the booths was Ali. He's new to town. Maybe Sadie knows him," said Asher.

"Who is Ali?" asked Ms. Caster.

"Ask Sadie. She might know his story since he told us he's from Lebanon. We just met him."

"Please discuss this theft with the other employees, and if any of you think of anyone else, let me know. Thanks, boys. I wonder why no one took money from your tills?"

Ms. Caster headed to her office, scratching her head and furrowing her brow. *I've always been a trusting person, but now I'm suspecting everyone.*

Mike and Asher wondered also. "You don't suppose someone is trying to make us look guilty since our cash boxes are intact?" said Mike.

"Hmmm. I was thinking the same thing. This could mean trouble. We'd better meet Ms. Caster tomorrow and go over the books. Something is amiss. Someone has stolen money, and we'd better be ready to prove it wasn't us," said Asher.

When Ms. Caster got back to her office, she called Sadie. "What do you know about Ali, Sadie? I understand that he came from your village in Lebanon."

"Who told you that, and why are you asking?"

Ms. Caster told Sadie about the thefts and how she was looking into any new people in town or out of town who visited the park in the past two weeks and seemed at all suspicious.

"Now it clicks. When he was questioning me at my booth today, I thought he looked familiar. It is Ali. I can't believe he has come to Pittman. I wonder why? If it is truly Ali, I don't think you need to worry about him," said Sadie. "When I was growing up, Ali lived on our block. He was one of four boys in the Astair family. He also had a sister, Bernie, who was my age and one of my best friends. Since her parents were used to boys, they gave her a boy's name, and she became quite the tomboy. We had some great silly adventures as we grew up. When we were about five, Bernie and I used to play 'Snatch'. We would sneak up on one of her brothers and behind his back, Bernie would grab one of his toys while I would hiccup and dance around to distract him. I'm sure the boys were wise to us but allowed the charade because they saw how naïve we were and how much Bernie and I were enjoying our prank."

"What happened to Bernie? Did she come to Pittman with Ali?" asked Ms. Caster.

"I worry about what happened to her. We lost track of each other when the ISIS followers started raiding our villages." Sadie trailed off, pausing for a second. "I'm not sure why he came to this city. I'll follow up on this."

Ali came into Sweet Indulgences the next day. "Ali," Sadie said, "I didn't recognize you at Jiminy Peak. When did you get to Pittman? Sit down and have some ice cream. We have a lot to talk about."

When I asked him about coming here, he just gave me some lame excuse about knowing I was here and wanting to see how I turned out as an adult. I asked him how his family was, but he was vague and changed the subject. I expressed my concern about Bernie, but he said he didn't want to talk about her."

Ms. Caster asked, "Do you know how Ali got into the country? Do you think he is here illegally?"

"If he didn't have a sponsor, I asked him how he got into the country. He abruptly changed the subject, ignoring my question. Something has changed about him. I wonder what happened? I always liked Ali. He was a handsome and talkative boy, who treated Bernie and me kindly, but now he seems surlier and quieter than happy and gregarious, but I don't think Ali's a thief. I really don't know how or why he is here, but I don't think he is being truthful with me. I'll see what else I can find and get back to you."

"Thank you, Sadie."

****

Ms. Caster called Mike to report the conversation, asking him to fill in Asher. She wondered if Ali could be the thief. She also called Sheriff Houtman to report the possible theft and told him of their plans to audit the sales. "I hope the thief isn't one of the people I hired. I have always valued my ability to judge people," Ms. Caster told the sheriff. "If we find any evidence, I will inform you. I'm hoping this is all a mistake, but after the report of the stolen band instruments, I thought you should know, just in case we have a thief in our midst. You might want to ask Sadie about Ali Astair, who recently moved here from her village in Lebanon. Sadie knows him from her past, but he might be here illegally."

"I'll talk to Sadie. Keep me informed of any further developments," said Sheriff Houtman. "Meanwhile, I'll send Deputy Murphy over tomorrow to discuss with

Mike and Asher what they have found out about the thefts."

"Thank you, sheriff, it's good to know you support the local businesses."

Chapter 4

Security Problems

The last day of the Adventure Park season dawned bright and sunny with a chill in the air. Everything looked so enticing for this celebration. I was sure the tourists and the locals would have a wonderful time. I wandered around and saw lines at all the food booths and rides. People were laughing and having a great time. Plus, they seemed to be spending a lot of money. Everyone in town will benefit from their generosity.

Ms. Caster had hired Mr. Brump to help out with security. She didn't want any more money stolen.

Two problems did arise to complicate matters. At the motorcycle ride, one of the local teenagers fell off his bike. Wayne immediately called the squad, and the EMTs told the parents they were transporting their son to the hospital to be treated for a possible fractured elbow.

Wayne and Billy were devastated as the frustrated father shouted, "You two should be more responsible. I hope you have good insurance."

His wife tried to calm him down as Billy whispered to Wayne, "I don't think our insurance will cover accidents off the store's premises. We're in trouble."

"Don't worry, Billy, I think we're covered. I'll get Mr. Samuel Habbib, the lawyer, to help us."

The other problem was discovered by Ms. Caster, and she had Mike and Asher review the day's receipts. Saturday night, as they were tallying up the profits from the sales, they meticulously went over the profits. If there was evidence that the thefts were continuing, they needed to alert Mr. Brump, whom she had hired as head of security. They were upset when they discovered quite a discrepancy between the estimated take and the actual amount of money counted from several of the money boxes.

"Has the thief struck again? We need to hurry up and report this to Mr. Brump before Ms. Caster thinks that one of us is responsible for stealing."

Mike went to find our head of security while Asher stood by the money boxes to guard against any further theft.

"Mike, how much money do you estimate is missing?" asked Mr. Brump.

"If our calculations are correct, about five hundred dollars."

"Are your calculations correct? Could the estimates be wrong?"

"I don't think so. We know the number of booths, so the amount turned in for the fees is correct. The merchants each gave us a tabulation of how much they sold. We check the percentages they turned in and figure again the percentage owed. Then we recount the money we took in from each raffle and the motorcycle rides. Here are our calculations," said Asher.

"Wow," said Mr. Brump. "That's about ten percent of the take that's missing. I'm going to start questioning the merchants before they finish packing up their leftover merchandise.

"I'm going to call Deputy Murphy and have him help me out. He can check out all the raffle workers. Asher and Mike, you try to find out if anyone was loitering around by any of the money boxes. We'll meet back here in an hour."

Mr. Brump added, "Mike, before you start canvassing, you should give me the calculation sheets and money so I can have Ms. Caster secure them under lock and key."

Chapter 5

Suspected Thieves

Asher and Mike related to Deputy Murphy the details of the thefts at the Adventure Park.

Deputy Murphy asked, "Who would have motive and opportunity?"

Mike said, "Certainly, any of the people collecting money at the rides or booths could slip some of the cash into their pockets before locking their tills. Those at the display tables and food booths also handled large amounts of cash."

"But they all had to report their sales, so if it was one of them, why didn't they just under-report their sales? That way, no one would notice the missing money?" Asher asked.

"You're right. What did you boys find out about suspicious people walking around the Park?" Murphy asked.

Asher said, "I spotted Ali looking over his shoulder as he approached several booths. Milo stayed later than he needed to, and several people saw him wandering around the booths, and I'm not sure why. Wayne hung back supposedly to discuss their insurance with Mr. Samuel Habbib, the lawyer, but he left immediately before the Adventure Park closed. Also, Mr. Omar Habbib said he was looking for his son, Ahmram, but he was already in their car. I saw him as I went to the office."

Asher said to Deputy Murphy, "Do you know that Mr. Nelson has been verbally and physically abusing Milo? Milo was sobbing one day at school, and I saw him and asked if I could help. He said that no one can help him. Then he told me how his dad even threw a snake at him the other day when he was shouting at Milo for some little thing he did wrong. What kind of father would throw a boa constrictor at his son?"

Deputy Murphy asked, "Do you know if his dad has hit him?"

"Yeah," Asher said. "Milo said he gets a beating almost daily. I've never noticed any bruises so he must cover them up,"

Deputy Murphy asked, "Has he reported this abuse to the authorities?"

"No," said Asher, "he's too scared of what Mr. Nelson might do to him."

"But why would he steal from the Adventure Park? That's a motive for many things, but not stealing," said Mike.

"I need to get this additional information to Sheriff Houtman," said Deputy Murphy.

****

When the sheriff went to talk to Sadie the next day, she was meeting with the Super Sleuths. He filled them all in about whom Ms. Caster suspected was responsible for the theft of money from the cash boxes.

Sadie objected to his choice of suspects. "I'm sure Milo would do no such thing. What would be his motive? He's just a hardworking kid. Ali wouldn't steal either. I know him from my village in Lebanon. He's a good person. Look for someone else, Sheriff."

Sheriff Houtman left before the Super Sleuths also started telling him he was wrong. He would be questioning Milo Nelson and Ali later, but now he intended to go to Nelson's Pet Shop and question Horatio and his employees about the snake-throwing incident that had been reported to him. *And I naively thought life in Pittman would be so much calmer than Boston.*

No one was wild about Mr. Horatio Nelson because he was too hostile with customers and with his employees, but no one, as far as the Sheriff knew, wished him ill. He came to town last year and bought the former real estate office when Ferguson was arrested. Nelson converted it into Nelson's Pet Shop. Ironically, he specialized in various varieties of snakes. It seemed appropriate since Ferguson has been such a slippery snake. The Farley Street Merchant's Organization had several merchants looking into Horatio Nelson's past. They didn't want to be blindsided like they were when Ferguson and Tyler came to Pittman with their hidden, shady pasts.

The sheriff questioned some of Nelson's employees while Nelson was dealing with a customer. One of the employees told the sheriff that he had observed the whole scene. When Mr. Nelson opened his pet shop, he checked all the cages, then frantically yelled, "What happened to B.C.?" All the employees stopped in their tracks and stared at Mr. Nelson. He was carefully lifting the lid of the twenty-gallon aquarium tank. The bottom of the tank was filled with stones and should have housed a twelve-inch, gray slitherer named B.C. (Boa Constrictor).

Another employee reported that Mr. Nelson had shouted, "Milo, get in here, now!"

Milo, Mr. Nelson's meek son, had shuddered and said, "Oh no, now what did I mess up?"

The same employee told the sheriff that Milo had worked at Nelson's Pet Shop since it opened. Never one to look for trouble, trouble seemed to follow him constantly. All the employees knew that he hated working for his ill-tempered father, and told the sheriff that Milo complained incessantly about not being paid enough.

Another employee told the sheriff he had witnessed Mr. Nelson's violent display of temper. He mentioned that Nelson looked like a lion about ready to eat his prey, namely, Milo Johnathan Nelson. This was the scene the employee witnessed:

"Milo," Horatio Nelson had screamed, "yesterday, when you closed the shop, did you or did you not hear me say to put B.C. carefully into the silver aquarium tank next to the parrot's cage and lock the tank?"

Milo stammered, "Ye..Ye...Yes, sir! I heard you."

"Then where is he?" seethed Horatio. "Is he invisible? Does he have an invisibility cape? Did you put him in a rocket to space?"

"Um, um, um," said Milo.

"Um, um, um," repeated Corporal Feather, the interfering parrot perched next to the aquarium tank. Corporal Feather had the annoying habit of only repeating things when he could cause the most confusion. At any other time, if you asked him to repeat something, he stubbornly refused to say a word. That is why he hasn't been sold, even though he's quite beautiful. Customers expected a parrot to parrot what they said.

"Shut up, you useless parrot. Um, what, you blundering excuse for a salesman? Where is B.C.? A boa constrictor cannot, will not, must not be missing in Nelson's Pet Shop!" Mr. Nelson's face was so red, Milo thought he might explode.

Milo cringed. He would not stand there and listen to this rant. Just as he turned, his dad opened another aquarium, reached in, and grabbed another boa. In his anger, Nelson flung the snake at his retreating son. "Let's see if you can take better care of this boa. Now find B.C., you ingrate."

Milo fled to the back room. He dropped to the ground and rolled himself into a ball, cringing like a cornered animal.

Nelson was just finishing up with a customer, so the sheriff decided to return to the station to relay all the eyewitness testimony to Deputy Murphy. He will then come back and invite Horatio to come down to the station and explain himself.

Cameron Coldren saw the sheriff leave and came into the store, determined to confront Horatio about the scene he previously had observed as he was passing the pet shop. With a look of anger, he demanded, "What is going on?"

Mr. Nelson immediately went into damage control mode. "I'm sorry you had to see that spectacle, Cameron. My son was defying me by refusing to work. I also discovered some cash missing, and I think he stole it from the cash register. I will get to the bottom of this. No one steals from me or defies me." Nelson stood tall and stared at Cameron defiantly. Milo peeked through the door of the back room where he was working and watched the less-than-friendly confrontation.

"Nelson, I came in here to discuss some business with you. I'll be in town a few more days, so when you calm down, get in touch with me, and pull yourself together, or you will find yourself without your lucrative side business." The journalist turned and left, leaving the other employees gaping at Nelson.

Since he was a toddler, Milo has put up with his father's tirades. After this humiliation with the snake, coupled with his dad's constant abuse, Milo was more determined than ever to escape from his father's clutches. Since they moved to Pittman and opened Nelson's Pet Shop, Milo had begun to plot his escape.

After Mr. Coldren left the shop, Milo decided it was time. He feared Coldren. He had witnessed Coldren and his father having a violent disagreement in the past about money, and Milo surmised that Coldren hated his dad. When Milo saw him enter the shop today, he thought of warning his dad or notifying the sheriff of their sinister connection, but Milo knew he was too much of a coward to make a scene, and feared his father wouldn't appreciate any interference.

I'll just continue quietly plotting my escape. No one will be the wiser.

Chapter 6

The Barbeque

The sheriff intended to go to Sadie's barbeque, but he and Detective Murphy got bogged down in their search for the thief. At the barbeque, Mike told Sadie, Lola, and me about his dad's letter. He also told us that this was the first letter he had received from his dad since he went to prison, and Sam didn't even bother to ask how he was.

"I'm pretty hurt by my dad's neglect. Does he even have any interest in his own son? I know he's been abusive in the past, but he seemed so contrite when he went to prison that I hoped he had changed."

Lola couldn't help but interrupt. "Mike, be careful. My experience with a child abuser has proven to me that they repeat often, so you need to not be so forgiving. Sometimes they can't help themselves, or don't choose to change."

I wondered if this comment came from first-hand experience. I don't know much about Lola's childhood. Could her mom or dad have been abusive toward her?

Then Mike broke the silence and told us about his dad's proposal for the Bowling Alley. "What should I do? Do you think Mr. Habbib will be a good and trustworthy person to run the Ten Pins Bowling Alley until Dad gets home? I know he's hoping I'll take it over when I graduate, but when I turn eighteen, I plan to get a new start far away from Pittman. I'll hate to leave my friends, but I can't stand that Bowling Alley, and my dad's attitude convinces me that I need to find someplace new and start over."

I looked at Sadie with concern. I don't want to see Mike move away.

Sadie vouched for Mr. Habbib. "He has a passion for running his own business and helped his dad in their corner store all his teen years in Lebanon. He was my brother's age, and I often eavesdropped on our porch as they discussed their futures. Omar intended to have his own business, and they speculated what business would be best. My brother, Alex, didn't know what he wanted to do. 'I might just join the army,' he said, 'but I don't like what I am seeing with the buildup of the ISIS movement. I hope you can achieve your dream, Omar, but I'm fearful for both our futures. We might not be able to just do what we want. Others might dictate our futures.'"

Sadie wasn't sure what Alex meant since she was too young to be aware of the political situation in the Middle East. She just hoped Omar, whom she considered to be another brother, and Alex got to realize their dreams.

"He needs a job," Saide said, "and wants to be independent from his brother, the lawyer, who sponsored him for immigration to this country. Taking over your dad's Ten Pins Bowling Alley would be ideal because it gives him a chance to use his experience. Omar is personable and will relate well to all the customers. Maybe you could encourage your dad to go into the partnership with Omar."

Everyone agreed this sounded like a good opportunity. Mike agreed to pass on these recommendations to his dad.

I decided to turn the discussion away from Mike and to Sheriff Houtman. They would deal later with Mike's determination to leave Pittman.

I said to the group, "Do you think Sheriff Houtman and Deputy Murphy haven't come to the barbeque because they don't want to face the Super Sleuths? We all solved the last crime in our town because the sheriff was wrong and arrested the wrong suspect. Do you think Houtman and Murphy are avoiding us because the sheriff has probably already concluded that one of you boys committed the thefts? Of course, that's wrong, and he knows we always prove him wrong. We need to call Sheriff Houtman and ask him what evidence he has about the thefts, and tell him how incorrect his assumption about the boys is. I'll call him first thing tomorrow."

Just as we were ready to disband, in walked Sheriff Mark Houtman. Lola jumped up and escorted him to the Super Sleuths' table, where we all immediately went silent.

"Ladies and gentlemen," Mark Houtman said as he took a seat. He looked worried.

"Is anything wrong, Mark?" asked Sadie.

"This morning, I saw the strangest thing as I passed Nelson's Pet Shop," said the sheriff. "Through the window, I saw an enraged Horatio Nelson throw a snake at his son, Milo, so Milo ran to the next room, and then Cameron Coldren entered the store. Cameron and Horatio angrily burst into a fierce argument. I wasn't even aware that Cameron knew Nelson. This scenario seemed so strange that I thought before getting involved and bringing Horatio in for questioning, I would see what you all know about the two of them."

I couldn't believe that the sheriff was consulting the Super Sleuths about our opinions. Normally, he ignored us or told us to mind our own business. I wondered what was going on. The Sleuths jumped right in.

Sadie said, "I don't like Horatio Nelson because he is a bigot who hates and verbally abuses immigrants. I, myself, have experienced his verbal insults, and Mr. Habbib has told me how hostile Nelson is toward him and his son if they go into the store. It's a shame because Ahmram loves animals and doesn't understand why his father won't take him to visit the pet store. We also suspect him of putting up a sign in Mr. Habbib's yard that said, 'Foreigners not welcome here. Go back where you belong.'"

Lola chimed in next. "Nelson is slimy. He ogles the young women who enter his store. I don't know how he stays in business. Once was enough for me, and I know several young mothers who have stopped going there unless Milo is at the cash register. They don't like Nelson's attitude toward them and their kids. Sheriff, have you checked his background to see if he could be a pedophile or a philanderer?"

"This is the first I'm hearing of these accusations. We will look into it, be assured. Which brings me to why Nelson and Cameron were arguing. Cameron is a reporter. Do you think he has some knowledge of Nelson's seedy side?"

Asher jumped in, "Maybe you better ask Cameron, sheriff. I know that Nelson's son, Milo, is scared of his father. I think he abuses Milo, but I can't get Milo to confide in me. He just hints at the abuse. I know they don't get along."

Sheriff Houtman's phone rang, and after he listened, he said, "Thank you for your input. I have to cut this short. They need me back at the office, but between Deputy Murphy and myself, we will search Horatio's background and discuss Milo's fear with his teachers. Meanwhile, boys, keep an ear out for anything Milo might say about his dad. We will get to the bottom of this. I don't think any father should be so cruel as to throw a snake at his own son."

We all nodded in agreement.

Chapter 7

Planning for the Ski Fest

After the others left the barbeque, Lola and I stayed behind to talk about the opening of the ski season since we had volunteered to oversee the Welcome Ski Season Fest in November. Before everyone arrived for the planning meeting the next day, I called the sheriff but was told that he was at Jiminy Peak. I told the receptionist, "Please have him call me about the thefts before he sets his mind on the wrong suspect." I huffed to myself. *It's hard to get that man to listen to reason when he sets his mind on one person whom he has determined is guilty.*

The first scheduled meeting for the Ski Fest was at my Bookworm Shop at noon Sunday. This November event brought a huge crowd of skiers from all over the Berkshires. It started about five years ago, and the crowds had grown each year. Even if the snowfall didn't accumulate much, Jiminy Peak manufactured enough man-made snow to entice the skiers, and all who attend the Fest love to watch the colorful trees starting to turn brown as they shed their leaves.

The chill is in the air and skiers from all over the north shine up their equipment and purchase any new equipment at our well-stocked ski shop. Parents loved this shop because, for a small fee, they could trade in their kids' shoes and skis for bigger sizes, which saved them a lot of money.

As the committee members entered the Bookworm Shop, I called out, "Close the door quickly. The leaves are blowing all over. I don't want a windstorm of leaves inside the store."

In a good mood, the committee members trooped in. Lola and I were pleasantly surprised at the turnout. All dove into the refreshments before the meeting began and talked about the Fall weather and how the panorama of color that burst upon the town and surrounding mountains would soon disappear into a white landscape. Busloads of tourists had been arriving all week to view this Autumn spectacle. This was a real boon for the shop owners who depended on the tourist trade to boost their seasonal sales.

Those attending the meeting then gathered in a circle to get down to business and discuss their roles as volunteers for the Ski Fest. The Geezer Book Club was well represented by Edna Mae, dressed to the nines, high heels and all, jack of all trades, and considered the town gossip. Edna Mae at sixty-five-years-old was an experienced businesswoman and had become their book club's charismatic leader, and Mr. Brump, about seventy-one, was the resident grump,, balding, and not stylishly dressed. He looked like an aging Columbo with his trench coat and pipe. The Farley Square merchants sent Sadie, Billy, Wayne, Horatio, and Milo Nelson to represent the merchants' organization.

Sadie introduced the handsome Cameron Coldren to the group. "You all must be acquainted with this famous newsperson from Boston, who is planning to generate some needed publicity for our town. Mr.

Coldren is honoring our small town by featuring it in his popular Video Documentary Series."

"Oh, I've seen your wonderful documentaries, Mr. Coldren," oozed Edna Mae. "I felt like I was on a fantasy tour of places I've never seen. You make everything seem to come alive."

Everyone clapped enthusiastically as Mr. Coldren acknowledged their accolades. He greeted the committee. "I'm thrilled to meet everyone, and I can't wait to experience your Ski Fest. This is just the type of activity I was hoping to witness and feature in my documentary series focused on stories about small-town life in the Berkshires. I also will be interviewing some of your local citizens on my podcast to hear why they settled in Pittman, and how they like the small-town atmosphere. Maybe you can recommend people to interview."

Milo asked, "Gee, Mr. Coldren, did you grow up here? Do you live near here?"

"I live in Boston, and I grew up in a large city, young man, so I am happy to learn about small towns and showcase their unique place in our lives.

"This is Andy, my photographer. He would like to take some pictures with the background of the falling leaves. He's hoping to get some intriguing photos to enter a photography contest. Winning this contest could lead to a book contract for the winning photographer, who would then have his or her book published and receive regional New England distribution. The contest is showcasing the advantages of small-town living. Please feel free to share your many stories and pictures with me and Andy."

Lola said, "I'm a fan of photos of people of all

ages. Their faces can really reflect all the feelings of our world. They tell a story. I worked at a theater in Hollywood, CA. We did a play where all the scenery was just large photos of people's faces placed around the stage. I'd love to see some of your photographs, Andy."

Lola whispered to me, "I'd be happy to share stories or anything else with this reporter with the striking blue eyes, or even with his handsome photographer, especially over an elegant dinner and expensive drinks."

"Shhh," I said, "someone will hear you."

Lola giggled. In her twenties and gorgeous, Lola had an active imagination, especially when it had to do with romance. Now, her imagination went into high gear, and she whispered to me, "Think of my future with this famous newsman. Can't you just picture Cameron and me strolling along the Seine at the conclusion of our Mediterranean cruise, shopping in the exclusive shops of Paris as Cameron helps me pick out a perfect wedding dress embroidered with pearls? Finally, picture all of my friends from Pittman climbing the stairs of the Notre Dame Cathedral after their journey to attend our glorious wedding. Andy will photograph each step of the way unless he decides to steal me from Cameron and whisk me away to a mountain in the Swiss Alps."

I said, "Lola, come back, come back to reality. We need to assign the volunteers their responsibilities for the Ski Fest."

Lola and I went into manager mode and handed out jobs. "We'll organize the food booths," offered Sadie and Marie. Marie was a sumptuous baker, and Sadie would provide some of the popular dishes from Sweet Indulgences. My mouth was already watering. "We are so lucky to have such talented cooks," I said to the group of volunteers, then introduced Sadie and Marie to Cameron and Andy."

Wayne said, "We'll set up the displays for the businesses taking part, and Asher and Mike offered to handle the financial end of the Ski Fest from ticket sales to fees for booths, etc. Their interest in all things financial had been sparked by helping the band treasurer work with the band's accounts and Ms. Caster with the Jiminy Peak Adventure Park accounts."

Sadie said, "I'll volunteer to usher Mr. Coldren around the Fest and introduce him to all the locals."

Lola glared at Sadie as if she wanted to protest.

Edna whispered to Marie, "I don't trust anyone with his good looks. See how he has already charmed Lola and Sadie."

I overheard what Edna said and jumped into their conversation. "Now, let's not be spreading any rumors. I met Cameron Friday, and he seemed to be a reputable man. You know how dramatic Lola is, and I wouldn't deny Sadie a bit of hope in her life. The sheriff doesn't seem to be stepping up to the plate in the romance category."

I understood Edna's concern. I also was a little worried about Lola and Sadie's seeming fascination with the handsome, charismatic journalist.

I thought, *This better not end up being a competition between Sadie and Lola for Cameron's affections.*

When everyone had an assigned job, and just as the committee was about to adjourn, the elusive Sheriff

Houtman, followed by Deputy Murphy, entered the store. Sheriff Houtman said, "Sorry we're late, but I think you will need to have a group handle security at the Fest. You may not be aware that we have had some burglaries and thievery take place in our small town. The band room was vandalized, and several valuable instruments were stolen. Also, I've just met with Ms. Caster, Jiminy Peak's manager. She reported thefts of cash the last few weeks that the Adventure Park was open. We don't want to tempt a thief with sloppy security. Deputy Murphy and I will try to be present that day, but in case of other duties arising, we will need an on-site head of security."

Some volunteers seemed quite shocked at this turn of events. I could see a light go off in Cameron's eyes. I hope he won't focus on crimes in our city. We want him to sing our praises to attract swarms of tourists. That's the only reason I agreed to this video.

People started questioning the sheriff, but he deflected all the questions and said, "I'm not prepared to answer questions until a further investigation is completed."

Mr. Brump, the Grump, stood up and surprised us all by saying, "Sheriff, I'll take the job as Head of Security. I used to be a detective before I retired, so I think I can keep us secure. I also just worked a few days at the Adventure Park as Chief of Security. I didn't realize how much I missed being involved."

Relieved, we all clapped, except Cameron, who scowled. Mr. Brump seemed to uncharacteristically smile.

"Now, why didn't I know he's a former detective? I wonder how his grumpy personality suited that job?"

said Edna Mae to her cohort, Beth. "I bet he scared prisoners into confessing after they got one look at his expression and heard his grumpy questions. I need to talk to Robin. Mr. Brump hasn't been forthcoming about his background since he joined our Book Club in April. I asked around town at that time, but no one seemed to know anything about him, except that his wife had been sick, and he had cared for her until she passed away."

In a whispered aside, I told Lola, "I don't like the look on Cameron's face. I hope Cameron doesn't have anything to hide. We really don't know much about him. He looks like he is leery of the grumpy retired detective. I'm sure he intends to get Mr. Brump's story. I guess we all would like to hear that story. Maybe he'll interview him on the podcast."

I was pensive, then shook my shoulders and proceeded to tidy up the room as everyone was leaving. The Geezer Book Club was relatively new. A few months ago, they requested to host their book club at my store. I am glad I agreed. They meet twice a month to discuss the books they pick. Everyone is supposed to choose one book, many of which I suggested from my inventory, then I make a list, and Edna Mae sets up the schedule.

There are four women and three men. Edna Mae was well dressed and had been referred to by Lola as Ms. Lawyer, Ms. Defender, and Ms. Organizer. Her type A personality made her the natural self-appointed leader of the group. For each meeting, she handed out a biography of the author and a list of questions for discussion. Beth was the peacemaker in the group, and if any discussion got too hot, she would steer it back on track. We all appreciated Marie, our creative baker because she baked inventive cakes and tasty cupcakes, which she brought to each meeting.

Bart O'Neal was our researcher and teacher. A plus in his favor was that he was a master griller and often brought in some delicious ribs to sample. Besides discussing books, we shared a penchant for good food, and greedily consumed any treats members brought in. Harley and Gramps were complete opposites. Harley was the debonair, elegant, and intellectual type who managed to eat a barbeque rib without getting a drop of sauce on his fingers, chin, or shirt. Gramps dove into all the food with relish. He was everyone's friend and watched over us like a grandfather. That's how he earned the nickname Gramps. He made me miss my dad and grandpa, and Lola loved his kind personality.

As everyone was getting ready to leave, Edna Mae came up close and cautioned me. "Robin, you better keep an eye on Sadie. She seems to like Mr. Coldren. If the sheriff finds out, he will be jealous. Also, I think Lola likes Cameron too, so this might cause a rift between Sadie and Lola. You are a good negotiator and should step into this situation right away before things get out of hand. We don't know much about this journalist, and we don't need discord in our pleasant town. I predict that trouble is a-comin'." I recognized Edna Mae's concern, but I didn't need to get in the middle of a love triangle.

After speaking her piece, the busybody turned around and started to leave. Just then, the door opened, and a stranger walked in. Everyone turned and stared at him.

I looked and practically fell off my chair. Asher

stared at me. Then I ran to the stranger and embraced him. Asher stared. Suddenly, he too ran to join in a group hug. We were laughing and finally turned to the astonished committee members.

"I would like you all to meet a dear friend, Mr. Matt Clare from Kentucky, my husband John's best friend and mischievous instigator of grandiose schemes. We've been talking over the phone about a visit, but I thought he meant in the winter, not now. What a great surprise."

Lola stood up and welcomed Matt, then turned to the members of the planning committee. "You've all done a wonderful job. I think we're ready for the Ski Fest. Now, finalize the details. You all have plenty of time until November, but let's get ahead of any deadlines. If you have any questions, you can ask Robin or me. The setup will be the Wednesday after Halloween in the afternoon and evening, and the fest begins the Friday night after Halloween at six. See you all there. The only committee that still needs to finalize plans is security. Mr. Brump, Sheriff Houtman, and Deputy Murphy will meet with Robin, me, Mike, and Asher to finalize their plans, and we will inform the whole committee of the details. Thanks to all." Lola did a silly dance and bowed to all as her finale. All clapped and went on their merry way, chattering away curiously looking at Matt, Asher, and me.

Chapter 8

Matt and Robin

Matt and I couldn't stop talking. We were so excited to see each other. Asher just stared at Matt and smiled. I knew he was thinking of his dad fondly.

I asked, "Matt, why are you visiting our small town?"

Asher interrupted, "Mom, Matt, I need to go to band practice. Will I see you tomorrow, Matt?"

"You'll be seeing me a lot, young man."

Asher left floating on the cloud of his memory of his dad and Matt, his best friend.

Matt looked intensely at me and said, "I have an idea for a project I've been working on, and I wanted to run it by you in person to see if it is plausible. It's time for me to slow down, and I have fond memories of the visits to the Berkshires with my wife and you and John. After Ella died of cancer three years ago, I was at loose ends. I threw myself into my work at the Playhouse and drowned my sorrows. With the help of a psychiatrist friend, I decided I needed a meaningful project to ease into retirement.

"That's when I decided to maybe pull up roots and move here if you think the project is worthwhile. There's no replacement for a friend's honest opinion."

Matt continued to explain to me that when he

began making plans for his semi-retirement, he considered northern Kentucky or Cincinnati, but the theater scene in Cincinnati and Louisville are saturated. "I got this inspiration as I was watching a new spectacular event in Cincinnati called the 'Bling Festival.' As the lights flashed, and everyone swayed to the music, I thought, '*Matt, it's now or never.*'

"I went back to my studio at the Cincinnati Playhouse and wrote and dreamed and wrote some more. Ideas shot through my mind like the lights at Bling, and the result after weeks of dreaming was a specific plan for going forward."

"Oh, Matt, you always were the idea man. John would follow any of your ideas, crazy or not."

We laughed, thinking of my husband.

"Matt, remember the first time you and John took me to a Bluegrass festival in Devou Park in Covington? We were seated on blankets with Ella and our neighbors, and I was astonished when suddenly everyone would whoop and holler and clap loudly, then silence, then a few minutes later, cheers again. I asked Ella why everyone was cheering and carrying on. She said, 'That was a particularly difficult chord sequence the fiddler just performed.' And everyone except me recognized the difficulty. I knew then that I was out of my comfort zone."

"Robin, that's what I'm looking for–the wow factor," Matt said. He proceeded to outline a plan for a Children's Theater right here in Pittman. "I could commission scripts, gather local playwrights, and actors, and form a company. We'll need a director, but I can handle all aspects of production. What is your honest opinion of this crazy idea?"

"Will you move here permanently or just for the summers?" I asked.

"Permanently. It will take year-round work to be successful. I can recruit some of the actors and directors who come in the summer."

"Matt, I honestly think this theater will complement all that Shakespeare and Company and the community theaters offer. New York and Boston actors and directors come to the Berkshires for summer stock and might also be interested in your project."

Matt surprised me and reached over, grabbed me, and swung me around chanting, "Here we go again. Dreaming, and dancing, and creating!!"

I was out of breath after this enthusiastic display. I hardly had time to think. Things were moving so fast.

"Wait a minute, Matt. Take a deep breath. Let's give this idea a chance to settle. Where are you staying?"

"At the Berkshire Mountain Lodge."

"Good. Take some time to think this all through. Tomorrow, take a trip down Route 7 to the Pittman Forest. Walk in silence and think, plan, create. You can't just jump into this on a whim. Whatever you do is going to affect your family life and the lives of children in our community. I'll meet you tomorrow night at the Swan Inn for dinner. Then, we can talk further. Ryman Farm has a great fireworks display that we can watch after dinner and then revisit all of your plans."

"Okay, I know you're right, but I'm just so excited." Matt smiled, clapped his hands, kissed me on the cheek, and saluted goodbye as he headed to his motel.

Chapter 9

Can He Make It Work?

At dinner the next night, Matt and I reminisced about the beautiful Kentucky horse farms. I related a story of when Dave was little and wanted to ride a horse. John and I went to the Kentucky Horse Farm, and Asher rode a pony and practically fell off. Matt tells me about his kids' adventure at Camp Ernst summer horseback riding camp. They loved it and conquered their fear of the large creatures. They even learned how to groom a horse, which proved useful for one of his sons who took a summer job at one of the many Kentucky horse farms on the way to Lexington, Kentucky.

I reminded Matt of a time when he and his wife accompanied my family to Bardstown, Kentucky, for the *Stephen Foster Story*. We both remembered the beautiful period costumes and the soaring voices of the college students from the local theater programs.

When Ryman Farm began its fireworks display, Matt and I shared stories of the magnificent fireworks display on the Ohio River. The best seats were at Reds' stadium and the hill at Devou Park.

After a lovely evening filled with memories and laughter, Matt told me of his decision. "I did as you said and walked in the forest and thought and thought about the theater project. I found myself so excited to start the planning. This has given me a sense of purpose again. I need to resurrect my enthusiasm. I'm not quite ready to retire yet, and I think this is the way to use my talent productively. An added incentive is being near you and Asher again. My boys have been anchorless since Ella died of cancer. They will love it here and reconnect with their best friend, Asher. There are a lot of colleges in the New England area, so that would give them options besides the University of Louisville and the University of Kentucky. I can't wait to bring them up here soon to see if they like the high school and the area. It's hard to transfer in your senior year, but I think it will be a good move for all of us. I value their opinions and want to see them happy again."

"Think about it, and maybe you could take a quick weekend trip to Kentucky to see your old friends and tell the boys about the things there are to do in the area."

"I'll certainly think about it all. I want to discuss this idea with Lola, my actress friend, to see what she thinks. I'll call you next week. For now, I need to pack it up and turn in. I'm exhausted. Good luck with all your decisions. Come to a farewell dinner tomorrow with Asher and me so we can properly send you back to Kentucky. Thanks so much for coming. This visit has been a delightful surprise. I missed you so much."

****

After the fest planning meeting, Lola left the bookstore and went to the town square. She sat on her thinking bench as the cool breeze invaded her lightweight jacket, and leaves blew around like a flock of colorful butterflies. She couldn't enjoy the scene because her mind was reeling, and she was afraid that someone would discover the one secret that she had never shared with anyone.

After Mr. Brump announced that he was an ex-cop from Chicago, Lola flinched. Mr. Brump was staring at her. Lola had first met him in Grant Park in Chicago. She recognized him when he first came into the Bookworm Shop. She didn't think he recognized her then. Did Mr. Brump recognize her now?

Lola remembered it well. *Mr. Brump was one of the officers present when I went to Grant Park to identify my mom's body. Now I'm in trouble. Does he have any idea about my secret?*

A few weeks before Lola's mom died, she insisted that Lola meet her for lunch at their favorite Greek coffee shop on Division Street. When they were halfway through their salad and lemon chicken and rice soup, Lola's mom whispered to her, "Lola, I have something very important to tell you. Now, listen carefully. If anything happens to me, I need you to go immediately to my apartment. In the middle drawer of the hutch under the placemats and napkins, you will find a yellow envelope. Take the envelope, leave my apartment, and go somewhere private. When you get there, open the envelope. Inside you will find some money. Take it and deposit it in your own account. Do not tell anyone where you got it.

"But, Mom," Lola objected, "you seem perfectly healthy. What's wrong? Please tell me. You're worrying me."

"I'm fine. Don't worry. This is all legal. It's money I've saved over the years from my performances with the band and sales of our CDs. The only illegal dollars are the ones from when I sold drugs. I refused to use that money even though I needed it. I was in too deep to my supplier to stop selling drugs, but I finally made a choice to at least do something good with the money. Whatever I could put aside, I saved for you. Take the money and use it for your acting career. No one knows about the cash, so take it and do something good with it."

Lola was stunned. Her mother had always seemed to be living from paycheck to paycheck, and now she was talking about money saved. Curious, Lola asked her mother, "How much money are you talking about?"

Her mom turned away just as the waitress approached their table to see if they wanted dessert. Mom asked for the check. "I need to leave now, but remember if anything happens to me, go right to the hutch, stash the money in your purse, and head right to the bank."

Three weeks later, on a windy Chicago day, Lola got that fateful call from the police to come to the park because her name was found as a contact person on a card in a deceased woman's handbag.

That is where Lola met Officer Brump when he pulled aside the sheet that was covering her mom's body. Without a sympathetic word, he said, "I need you to identify this body and tell me what you know about this person."

"This person? This person! What happened to her? You are talking about my mom, not some mannequin, you hateful, unsympathetic pathetic robot."

Mr. Brump must have recognized me at the bookstore.

I wonder if he remembers me calling him a robot?

Is it possible he knows about the money from my mother?

Lola intended to use that money as her mother wished. That's where she got the down payment for her acting studio so she could further her love of acting.

Another secret kept from Robin. Now what? Will Mr. Brump spill the beans?

Chapter 10

Trouble at Finnegan's

Friday night, Cameron and Andy, his photographer, went to Lennon to Finnegan's, the only nearby bar since Ten Pins is still closed in Pittman.

Andy slammed down in a chair, balled up his fists on the table, and asked angrily, "Geesh, Cameron, what's your problem today? You sneered at that girl, Lola, who's obviously enamored of you. Then you snapped at me when I asked you to pose with Lola and Robin. They are the organizers of this festival, you know. I can't imagine why you would want to alienate them. You also looked guilty as all get out when the sheriff appointed Mr. Brump the head of security. What on earth were you thinking? Is there something I need to know? Do you know Mr. Brump?"

"Andy, just leave me alone." The waitress appeared and set the steins down on the table. Cameron immediately chugged down his beer. "I have a lot on my mind. It's like I never get a moment to myself."

"Well, you're going to have a lot of moments to yourself if you don't get your act together."

"What's that supposed to mean?" Cameron took another long drink from his stein, called the server for another round, and glared at Andy.

"I saw you last night drinking heavily with Horatio

Nelson, the pet store owner. Did you know him before you came to Pittman, or can you just naturally spot a fellow drinker? Nelson didn't look pleased with you. In fact, he looked like he would haul off and hit you at any minute. You better be careful. This is a small town, and word travels quickly. Someone will comment on your excessive drinking, and your reputation as a standup journalist will go down the drain. I've also overheard some gossip that many people in this town don't like Mr. Nelson. You shouldn't be seen as his drinking buddy. You can't get into trouble and then just disappear into the shadows like you do in the big city. Did you ever think that if you ruin your reputation, it affects mine also? My career, at the moment, is tied to your success."

Cameron just growled at his photographer and then stomped away.

Andy slumped down at the bar table, deep in thought. Cameron is his best friend, but Andy knew that he had a dark side that he mostly kept hidden, but the last week was bad. Nothing seemed to please Cameron. He was on the phone constantly, and when Andy approached, he either hung up or walked away. *I wonder what Cameron's secret is?* Andy cast a worried look around the bar.

Cameron has had a few notable failures lately, and his boss is upset. We need a win with this feature on small towns versus big city living. His win is my win. He better not leave me in the lurch. Friend or not, I don't intend to take the fall for his misdeeds. I need to know why he's so nervous and cranky. My future is tied to his star, and I don't intend to be a falling star.

Andy looked up and spied Lola at the table by the

window, deep in thought. He decided he needed a little distraction from his own furious thoughts, so he approached the lovely Lola.

Lola looked up as Andy approached her table. The handsome photographer asked, "Do you mind if I join you? I could use some company."

Andy and Lola ended up talking for a long time. They discovered that they shared a love of acting and big city living, she in Los Angeles and Chicago, he in New York. They reminisced about their prior lives, talked about their successes and failures, and related the details of some of the stupid things they had done at the beginning of their careers.

"It feels good to laugh about my ridiculous mistakes," Lola said. "I remember one summer I was helping Jana with costumes at Shakespeare and Company. I put the wrong britches out for one of the cast. He was supposed to have a quick change and then snobbishly saunter onto the stage. Instead, he went on stage, pulling at his pant legs, and the pants started to fall down, then he had to hold them up as he pretended to be quite sophisticated. The audience dissolved in laughter. It was a disastrous but funny performance. Poor Jana got blamed for the mistake, and love that she was, she took the blame and never made me feel guilty."

Andy told Lola about the time he decided he had to go to the top of the Empire State Building to see the view. A kid of about seven looked at him in the elevator and said, "Mister, do you want to hold my teddy bear, Ralphy. You look scared. I used to be scared of elevators, but Ralphy helped me feel safe."

Andy and Lola enjoyed a good laugh and spent a

pleasant evening together. Andy asked Lola to meet him for dinner another night later in the week, and she agreed.

When she left Finnegan's, Lola had a big smile on her face. *It's nice to have several suitors who seem interested in me,* thought Lola. *I wonder if I should buy a teddy bear? I don't think I'll name him Ralphy, though. I'll name him Andy.*

****

The next day, I caught Lola staring out the window, lost in thought.

Lola was picturing different love scenarios. First, a wedding to Cameron on the beach on a tropical island, then a vision from Deputy Murphy driving up to her house with a limousine filled with bouquets, and last, but not least, Andy, the photographer, having her pose next to all the scenic sites in the Appalachian Mountains as they escaped on a week-long vacation.

Lola jumped when I spoke and laughingly revealed her daydreams to me. What an imagination.

"Lola, I'm leaving for my lunch with Sadie. Are you okay minding the store while I'm gone?"

"Sure, of course. Have a good time. If you think about it, would you bring me one of Sadie's great chocolate chip cookies? Also, if she's still selling those cute teddy bears she put on her gift shelf, will you please buy one for me, and I'll pay you back?"

"Will do. See you later. The next book, *The Rabbit Hash Mystery*, for the Geezer's Book Club is on the first shelf by the cash register in case Marie or Edna Mae come to purchase a copy."

"Got it. I'm awake and ready for action."

I wonder why Lola wants a teddy bear?

57

When I settled down at a table by the cash register in Sweet Indulgences, Sadie rang up a sale and then sat down to join me. I told Sadie more about Matt and some of the crazy things he and John used to do together, from camping adventures gone wrong because of hungry bears and a horseback trip where Matt fell off his horse while trying to stand on the saddle. Sadie and I laughed at the men's crazy antics.

"I miss their great pranks and humorous stories. I'm glad Matt came for a visit. We had such a good talk last night at dinner. He heads home tomorrow. I've missed him. At dinner, Asher started talking so fast because he was so excited to be with him. I'm sure Asher was reminded of how his dad and Matt were so funny together. Matt's off now to watch Asher perform at band practice. It'll be so good for Asher to have a father figure care about his activities. He'll miss Matt when he leaves. Asher will be thrilled if he and his boys decide to live here."

Switching the subject, I said to Sadie, "I wanted to discuss Lola with you. Have you noticed any changes in her moods lately? Before we opened this morning, I discovered her just sitting and staring into space in the storage room. She was so absorbed in her thoughts that she didn't even hear me come in. I asked her what was wrong, and she just told me about her silly daydream. Then, almost as an afterthought, she said she needed some time to talk to me about something personal. I would have invited her for dinner to discuss her problems, but Matt was coming over. I wish she would just give me a clue what this is about because I'm going to worry until we find time to meet."

Sadie said, "I'm glad you finally seem to have

someone in your life who you care for, and the neat thing is that you already know him so well, you seem so natural together."

"Now, Sadie, let's not jump to conclusions. He is leaving tomorrow and will come back with his boys to see if they like the high school and will be willing to transfer."

Sadie was a bit of a romantic, and I didn't need her imagining fictional scenarios for my love life.

Sadie said, "I know you will miss Matt. I hope his boys are willing to come. Maybe Lola's problem has something to do with this journalist, Cameron Coldren or Deputy Murphy. You remember what it was like when we were in our twenties. We all wanted to find our true love. Even when I was in the refugee camp, I wanted someone to love me. I used to go over the list of Alex's friends trying to picture a life together with one of them. I bet that's all this is. Do you want me to talk to her soon since you're so busy?"

"Oh, Sadie, would you please? I know she'll open up to you. You are so good at mothering these young people. They trust you and want your help with any of their problems. Look what you've done for Billy. He's turning into a confident young man, and that is partly your doing. Meanwhile, I'll try to find a time to talk to Lola after you talk to her. By the way, how are you doing with Cameron? How did your tour of Pittman go?"

"Just great. Cameron is such a charming conversationalist. He's interested in everything, the history of the town, each of the businesses on Farley Square, and he asked so many questions about the shop owners, particularly Billy and Wayne since they are about the youngest owners, and Mr. Nelson, since he's the oldest. You can tell he's a good journalist because of his curiosity about everything."

"I hope that's the only reason he's interested in the shop owners," I said. "I'm concerned that he might have a hidden agenda. It seems strange that he's able to stay in Pittman for such a long time. Doesn't he have a deadline for his video documentary series? I'm not so sure about him. I also think he might be a drinker. Some days he looks like he has a hangover.

"Did you know that Marie from the Geezer Book Club wants me to watch out for you because she thinks you and Lola might get into an argument as you fight for the affections of the same man, this charming journalist?"

Sadie just laughed. "You are both thinking about the wrong man. You know I only have eyes for a now jealous Mark Houtman. Maybe, just maybe, he has an interest in me. He was warning me to be careful about Cameron because no one seems to know much about him. I haven't seen any evidence that Cameron is a drinker or that he is in any way dangerous. Personally, I think the sheriff is just jealous, which I find truly enjoyable."

"Perhaps you will start getting bouquets of beautiful flowers too, like Deputy Murphy gives to Lola."

Sadie and I laughed about the men in our lives. We reveled in our now four-year friendship.

"By the way, you are invited to a birthday party tomorrow night," I said.

"Is it your birthday, Robin?"

"No, forty is enough. I don't need another birthday

for a long time. At our meeting of the Geezer Book Club, Marie invited us to help celebrate her eighty-fifth birthday. Since her husband died five years ago, and they had no children, we knew she was alone and yearned for friends to celebrate with her. She specifically asked that I invite you also."

Sadie said, "I would love to come."

"Okay, see you tomorrow night. Oh, I can't leave without a teddy bear for Lola. Do you have any more?"

"Sure, why does she want a teddy bear?"

"Who knows? Another secret for Lola."

Chapter 11

Birthday Surprises

Lola, Sadie, and I, plus the Geezers, attended
Marie's party. I offered to bring a cake, but Marie said
she had that covered. "Of course, you would. You make
cakes for a living. You'd think I'd realize that, but I'm
so tired today, I'm not thinking straight. How about I
just bring some snacks?"

"That's kind of you, dear, but you don't have to go
out of your way. I know you've had a very full schedule
lately," said kind Marie.

Lola said, "I'll be in charge of the entertainment."
Little did I know of the surprise Lola and Marie were
planning.

The boys had band practice the night of the
birthday party. Since Mike had just gotten his license,
he borrowed my car, and the boys intended to go out for
pizza after band practice.

Billy was going to join them since it was his night
off from the bike shop. He was tired of covering for
Wayne when he disappeared on these mysterious cash-
producing trips he had told the boys about. Asher told
me that he is worried about Billy. "He invested all of
his inheritance in this partnership partly because we
vouched for Wayne as a good guy. I don't know
enough about Wayne's mysterious trips, but I told Billy

to confront him. I don't know if Billy will or not."

Billy said, "I need a break, and even if Wayne is not there working, I'll join you."

I rode with Sadie to the birthday party and asked her about Wayne and Billy. I had seen a Closed sign in the window of the sales shop a little too often and wondered what was going on.

They were going to lose business if they closed too often.

Sadie filled me in. "Billy has complained to me about Wayne's absences. We're getting worried, but really haven't had time to act on any suspicions."

I vowed to make more time for the people I care about, like Billy. Changing the subject, I said, "I can't believe Marie is turning eighty-five. She's so intelligent and spry. I want to be like her when I grow up."

We laughed, and Sadie said, "We don't know much about her life before she moved to Pittman. She's a mystery to me. Do you know anything about her past?"

I said, "When she came to town about three years ago, she had just lost her husband and said she needed to find a new life. She was so sad in her New York apartment because everything reminded her of her husband. She moved here, bought a small ranch house, and looked around for something to occupy her time and use her energy productively. When she saw a small shop for sale on Farley Square, she bought it and decided that she would open a bakery since she had loved to bake all of her life. She must have money because she certainly didn't skimp on equipping the store.

"It wasn't long after she opened that word of her

unique bridal cakes and funny kids' birthday cakes spread. Within months, the store was a success. I think the best thing about opening the bakery was that she interacted so well with the locals, and she was quickly accepted into the community."

At the time, Marie had told me, "I don't feel like a stranger since I've met so many wonderful people in the community and the interesting tourists who flock in on the weekends. I'm glad I decided to follow my dream, and what an ideal place I picked."

"Other than her dream, I have no idea about her past life."

"Interesting," said Sadie. "We talk to people every day but never seem to get to know the whole person. Some people want to be anonymous, but I think we get so involved in our day-to-day business that we don't get to know others except on an artificial level."

As we pulled up to Marie's house, I said, "Sadie, I didn't know you were such a philosopher. You're right though. We go through life surfing on the waves rather than diving into the ocean."

We went into the quaint house and were greeted by all of the members of the book club. The fluffiest white cat I had ever seen immediately went in circles around me and waited until I sat down on the pristine white sofa then curled up in my lap. She nuzzled my hands so I would pet her.

"Oh, Queenie, leave Robin alone. Sorry, Robin, she's never met a person she doesn't like or seen as a petting machine. I call her Queenie because she thinks she's Queen of the Realm."

Lola asked everyone to be seated and announced, "Our entertainment tonight will delight you and amaze you. Edna Mae will be our emcee tonight." Lola bowed, and with a flourish, turned the program over to Edna Mae.

"Ladies and gentlemen, our program ranges from opera to comedy. Sit back and enjoy. Our first entertainer is our own birthday girl, Marie, singing a moving aria from *Aida*."

Marie stood up, looked fondly at us all, and began to sing in the most beautiful voice I have ever witnessed. When she blushed as she bowed to our standing ovation, she put up her hands to quiet us. "You are witnessing a solo from a former opera singer. I sang at the Metropolitan Opera, the Boston Opera Company, and toured over twenty cities in three years with the New York City Opera Company. Those were truly fulfilling years. I even sang with Beverly Sills at the New York City Opera. My husband was my biggest fan, and he became friends with most of the financial and publicity managers. I haven't performed since my husband's death. After his death, I went to New York, and Mark Jacobs at the New York City Opera was so kind to me. He reserved a seat for me in the center front, so that I could see one more opera before I moved. I cried that night, but I was determined to move on. I often sing in the privacy of my den. I decided I wanted to share this talent with you, my dear friends, at my eighty-fifth birthday party. Thank you all."

When we finally settled down again, Edna Mae announced, "For our second act, Mr. Brump, our lovable Grump, will perform a tap dance from his police academy talent show when he was a rookie cop."

"You've got to be kidding. Mr. Brump, a tap dancer?" I exclaimed to Sadie.

"Maybe we'll change his name to Fred Astaire or the Dancing Detective," said Sadie.

Stunned into silence, we watched Mr. Brump saunter onto the stage, dressed in plaid pants, a colorful shirt, and a top hat. He then performed an exciting tap dance routine. Next came Bart O'Neal, our researcher and teacher, who became Mr. Neal, the Science Guy, then proceeded to sing the periodic table in Animaniac style, speedily singing all the state capitols and continents, as everyone tried to sing along. We all dissolved in laughter.

"Now, ladies and gentlemen, I direct your attention to Mr. Roger's neighborhood featuring a modern-day Mr. Rogers, with a guest appearance by Captain Kangaroo."

Who would imagine that Harley, the debonaire and elegant man that he is, could wear a cardigan sweater and perform Mr. Rogers, getting ready to welcome everyone to the neighborhood. When he then welcomed Captain Kangaroo, here came Gramps, telling a modernized fable of the ant and the lion. Mr. O'Neal gave another animaniac performance as he sang as fast as possible a song about each person. It began, "This is Marie, who is not so old, and Robin, everyone's mother, and Sadie, our escapee, etc." until we all laughed like hyenas.

I turned to Lola. "Who knew we had such talent in our small town? Thank you for organizing this performance."

Edna Mae said, "Just a reminder, be sure to catch Lola's opening performance as the Shrew at Shakespeare and Company. She appears every Friday, Saturday, and Sunday, and I'm sure she will wow the audience. I hope you enjoyed everyone's performance."

At that point, Gramps carried in a marvelous cake decorated with musical notes and flowers. We quickly filled our plates and sat down to eat, laugh, and visit.

I was just biting into Marie's luscious chocolate birthday cake when Marie's landline and my cell rang. Lola picked up the landline and said, "Oh, no. Robin, answer your phone, now."

I panicked and said, "Hello, this is Robin George."

The sheriff said, "Robin, there's been an accident, but the boys are all okay. Your car, not so much. The EMTs need your permission to have Asher get some stitches in his forehead, but don't worry. It's just a slight cut. Since you are Mike's guardian, they also need your permission to take him to the hospital to get checked out."

"Yes, yes, of course. What about Billy?"

"Is Sadie with you?"

"Yes."

"Put her on."

"Sadie, there's been a slight accident. Only the car is hurt, but the EMTs need to take the boys to the hospital just to check them out. As Billy's guardian, they need your permission."

"Yes, of course. Robin and I will meet you there."

We explained to everyone and headed to the hospital. "Sadie, do you want me to drive? You seem so nervous."

"No, I'm okay. Do you think the sheriff is giving us the whole story? If they aren't hurt, why do they need to go to the hospital?"

"I'm sure it's just routine."

Sadie made the ride to the hospital in ten minutes

time, a record. We signed the required permission forms and were there as the sheriff interrogated the boys about how the accident happened.

Mike said, "This red car just came speeding right out of nowhere and was going to hit us head-on. Luckily, I instinctively swerved and then went over to the shoulder, but not before the driver swiped the side of our car. We came to rest after crashing into the guardrail. I think that's when Asher cut his forehead. They didn't even stop to see if we were okay."

"Did any of you see who was in the car or get a license number?" asked the sheriff.

"It looked like there were two people in the car in the front seat, but it was too dark to see who they were," said Billy.

"The red sports car looked like Cameron Coldren's, but I couldn't be sure," said Mike.

"I must have banged my head right away because I don't remember anything except the noise of our car crashing against the railing," said Asher.

The sheriff said, "Okay, boys, just go home and rest. If you think of anything else, you can call me in the morning, or have Robin or Sadie call me."

"Can we go to school on Monday?" asked Asher. "We have a major history test in AP History, and our history teacher says it could determine how we score on the AP History exam."

"We'll ask the doctor," I said. "He'll probably let you, if you feel okay."

When Mike and Billy went to bed, I couldn't sleep, so I called Sadie. I knew she wouldn't be sleeping either. "What do you think? Could the driver have been Cameron? I know the sheriff has had suspicions about him all along. He doesn't trust him, and I don't think it's just because he's jealous. Who would the passenger be?"

"I hope not," said Sadie. "I have enjoyed Cameron since he's been in Pittman. Do you think the passenger could be his photographer, Andy? Why would they be speeding down a road and fail to stop to see if anyone was hurt? If it was Coldren, he'll have to answer to me and see what the rath of the Lebanese means. Let's hope it was just some tourists joyriding."

I said, "I'll ask Lola. She's friendly with Andy. She told me they were together at the bar in Lennon the other night. I'll see what she says about him when she comes to work on Monday. We'll also see her at the play tomorrow. It will be interesting to see Deputy Murphy and the sheriff's attitude toward Mr. Coldren, since he is going with us to get a flavor of the theater scene in the Berkshires. If they think he drove the car that ran the boys off the road, I wonder if the sheriff will question him at the play? Try to get some sleep. I will also. I'll talk to you tomorrow."

Chapter 12

Should Shakespeare Be Revised

Sunday, we tried to bring some normalcy back into our lives as we all went to see Lola in *The Merchant of Venice*. The reviews were in from the dress rehearsal and said that Lola was a star shining brightly in the Venice sky, and one reviewer raved about the spectacular setting provided by crew members of Shakespeare and Company.

According to the same reviewer, the only flaw in the staging of this performance was the decision of the director to keep closely to Shakespeare's classic script. She thought that updating the production to fit our times would have been preferred by many modern women. *Kiss Me Kate* was a modernized production with music by Cole Porter. The reviewer enjoyed this production but would be glad for any modernization of the role of women, but she praised the performance of the actors. "The characters are great in both productions, and Lola does an exact portrayal of Katerina's temper tantrums and scheming. Petruchio was the perfect dominant suitor, but they could have revised the script enough to be palatable for the independent women of today."

Sadie, Mike, Asher, Billy, and I had seats together. We spotted Cameron and Andy on the other side of the theater, and Robert Murphy and Mark Houtman in the front row.

As the cast received a standing ovation after the show, Deputy Murphy went up on stage and presented a bouquet of daisies to Lola. She blushed and curtsied to him.

We all went to the foyer to wait for Lola to change and join us. We ordered drinks, wine and soft drinks, and cheese and cracker appetizers. Some ordered the delicious chocolate cake from Marie's bakery. Cameron, Andy, and Robert Murphy joined us. The sheriff had to leave since he was on duty, and though it was a quiet night, he had to catch up on paperwork. I think he was avoiding Sadie since Cameron was there, and Mark didn't want everyone to witness his jealousy. Besides, he did have a mystery to solve. Things were getting complicated, and he didn't seem any closer to catching the thief or thieves.

Asher started what became a heated discussion. "I can't believe they would produce such a play, Shakespeare or not, women must be incensed."

"You'd never get away with writing a play in this day and age that has women being tamed by a man and finally giving in to his insults and abuse, then happily marrying him," Mike chimed in.

"It's all in interpretation," said Cameron. "Kate is a strong woman. With a little tweaking of Shakespeare's script, she can be portrayed as in charge and scheming to trap Petruchio."

"Right, all it would take would be a few winks and asides from Kate and the whole dated tone of the play could be changed," said Asher.

"Hear! Hear!" said the boys and Cameron.

I held up my hands. "Now wait a minute. I totally disagree. When it comes to Shakespeare, I am a purist. I don't like it when they modernize the costumes, change the time period, or put in props that are anachronisms. Why, Sadie and I saw a play right here at Shakespeare and Company of Richard II where they had a scene, plotting the army's strategies on an iPad and calling on a phone to give instructions to those on the battlefield. How ridiculous."

Sadie said, "But, Robin, the audience found it hilarious and greatly appreciated the unexpected modern twist."

"I know, but I still stand by my opinion. Give me classic Shakespeare as it was written. Audiences need to realize that not all classics can be or need to be modernized. They need to realize what times in the sixteenth century were like during that historical period. I think knowing how women were viewed and treated in the past helps everyone appreciate and cheer the progress we have made in this century."

"Also," said Robert Murphy, "by viewing the play in the timeframe when it was written, you see the value and importance of family in the olden days. We often lose sight of families as units and the driving force of communities and towns, especially with children moving far from their parents. Sometimes, I long for a family cohesiveness."

"But what kind of cohesiveness is it if the father is the patriarch who dominates all decisions?" asked Andy.

Sadie chimed in. "You have no idea how a family works where the father is the dominant patriarch. I loved my father, though you would say he was a dictator who made all of our decisions for us. You are so wrong. If I wanted to go somewhere, and my father said no, I would tell my friends not to worry. 'Just give me some time.' I would then plan my defense. I would approach my father repeatedly with a different reason each time about why he should let me have the car. My father enjoyed arguing, and I knew in the long run, he would almost always give in and let me do whatever I wanted. He enjoyed the debate, and I understood that.

"My friends, who were not Lebanese, didn't understand how I didn't get angry at my father. In this play, Kate, too, understood how her father made decisions and was able to subtly work around them. This is a universal truth about women then and now. Women in the past just weren't so overt about their intentions."

I watched this heated debate, and then said, "I love that as a group, we can hold vastly different ideas and remain friends."

Asher said, "I wish all people today could do this."

"Yeah," said Billy. "Society today is so divided that many families avoid discussing any controversial subjects or leave in a huff if others don't agree with their opinions."

We all were quietly digesting this pathetic view of society today when Lola, glowing and holding bouquets of flowers from Deputy Murphy and Cameron, ran up to us, practically dancing and jumping for joy. "Well, what did you all think of the show?"

We threw aside any negative thoughts, hugged Lola, and lavished her with the praise she deserved.

"What a night!" I said as we headed to our cars.

"Thanks, Ms. George, for getting us all tickets,"

said Billy.

"I wonder who took Lola home?" said Sadie. "And if it was Cameron, what color car did he drive?"

We all looked pensive. No matter how happy we are, our fears keep rising, ruining our happy thoughts.

Chapter 13

Mysterious Wayne

Monday morning, Billy went in early to his bike shop. He told Sadie that he had some paperwork to catch up on. When he got to Hot Wheels, he pulled out all the ledgers and took a close look at the figures from the sales of motorcycles in August and September. The sales figures showed a dangerous drop in sales. August and September numbers were quite a bit lower than they should have been. The pleasant weather was prime time for motorcycle sales, so this downturn was troublesome.

When Billy tracked the daily sales, he realized, just as he suspected, that on the days when Wayne was in the shop, the sales were normal or better than normal, but his absence of eight days each month caused the decline. Because Wayne deposited a considerable amount of cash each time he returned from his trips, we, at least, weren't in the hole for each month.

"I need to confront Wayne about his absences," Billy told Sadie when he returned home. "I need to know where Wayne goes, and what he does to get all that cash."

"You're right, Billy."

"It's my business to, and my future. I can't cover for Wayne the days he spontaneously decides to close the showroom when I'm still in school. What if he is doing something illegal?" worried Billy.

"Let me know what he says after you discuss this with him," said Sadie. "I'll talk to Robin and see if she has any advice. She's a good businesswoman. Billy, if you find out Wayne is into anything illegal, don't try to handle it yourself. Talk to Sheriff Houtman."

****

When I left Sweet Indulgences Monday after breakfast, Sadie went back to work. In the kitchen, Sadie set up the industrial-sized mixer and started to get on with the baking.

She had several batches of bread to make for the afternoon crowd.

****

Mr. Habbib stepped into Sweet Indulgences without Ahmram in tow. He hoped to talk to Sadie. As the waitress led him to a booth, he spotted Sadie in the kitchen with her arms deeply immersed in a bowl, kneading a batch of bread dough. She reminded him of his wife who loved to bake. *Maybe it's time I started thinking about marrying again. Marlie would want that for me, and Ahmram needs a mother's love. After all, at thirty-five, I'm still young enough to enjoy having a family again.*

Omar asked the waitress to give a message to Sadie. "Please tell her that when she has a minute, I need to talk to her."

"Give me fifteen minutes," she told the waitress to tell Omar.

Omar Habbib ordered the kibbeh and pita bread. As he snacked on this treat, he anticipated savoring the delicious taste of one of his grandmother's favorite dishes, Koussa, which is stuffed zucchini. When the dish arrived, he wasn't disappointed. It was delicious.

As he ate, he daydreamed about his wife, Marlie. How he missed her kind looks, engulfing hugs, and motherly caresses for Ahmram. She was his life partner, his rock. Now, he felt so empty. He remembered her last days. Overcome with exhaustion and sickness from their days of hiding from ISIS, he had held her close and hoped and prayed she wouldn't leave him and their son. After four days of a high fever in that wretched refugee camp, Marlie succumbed, whispering, "Take care of Ahmram and yourself. I love you."

Wiping her floury hands on her apron, Sadie came over to his table, interrupting his thoughts. "Omar, you want to speak with me?"

"Sadie, I need advice. You have met Ali from our village. I knew his father, Mr. David. He came into my dad's corner store each week. His favorite purchase was lamb chops. He said his wife had a great recipe for lamb chops, and their son loved to eat them and suck all of their juice from the bones. Your brother, Alex, and I often worked with Ali on school projects.

"Well, I'm not sure how or why Ali is here in Pittman. He seems very much alone. Do you know why he is here?"

"Could he have traveled here with someone who subsequently abandoned him?" asked Sadie.

"I don't know, but Cameron was asking about Ali. I don't know if it was his journalist's curiosity, if he smelled a story to tell, or if he possibly had met him before. I didn't tell Cameron much because I don't trust him. Why would he be interested in Ali? Is he prejudiced toward Middle Easterners?"

"I don't think he has any prejudice toward foreigners," said Sadie. "He does seem to get a bit moody, though. When I introduced him to Mr. Nelson at the pet shop, he was unfriendly even though he had been friendly and charming to everyone else that day."

"Strange behavior," said Mr. Habbib. "Anyway, my question is, do you think I should offer Ali a temporary home with Ahmram and me until he can find a job and place to live? I spoke to him yesterday, and he was evasive about where he was living and why he was here. I saw him the other day coming out of the Pittman Forest with a sleeping bag. I suspect he has been sleeping in the forest."

"That would explain what I saw last week. I had several pies cooling on my window ledge, and one disappeared. The only person I saw was Ali at the end of the alley. Do you think he stole the pie because, not only is he homeless, but also hungry? I think he's been here about a week and hasn't yet looked for a job as far as I know. When he was passing my restaurant yesterday, I invited him in for ice cream. He seemed apprehensive, but he also looked hungry, so he came in and sat down. As we were both enjoying our sundaes, I tried questioning him. I asked if he had plans for the future. Of all the places to emigrate to, why pick Pittman? It seems strange. I had my aunt here, but he said that he didn't have any relatives."

"I've always liked him," Mr. Habbib said. "I felt sorry for him when I caught up with him walking down Rt. 7 from the forest. He seemed confused and a little lost."

Sadie said, "I feel for him too. He was so happy to eat a sundae. I would have liked to give him more food, but he was anxious to go. It seems like we are running Foster Homes of Pittman. Billy is living with me until he graduates; Mike is at Robin's while Sam is in prison, and now you want to take in a wandering young man from Lebanon as a roommate. I've heard of Pet Rescues, but we are dealing with People Rescues."

Sadie continued. "My advice to you is to take Ali to lunch or dinner here, and I will join you. Then we can question him together and get a feel for why he's here in Pittman, and what his needs are. Let me know when. I'm always here, and we have waitresses who help out several days at lunch and most evenings, so I can free up some time to join you."

"Thanks, Sadie. It's a date," Mr. Habbib said as he left.

Chapter 14

Hiding Out at the State Forest

The day that Omar had seen Ali come out of the State Forest, Ali had been sitting on the banks of Berry Pond at the top of Berry Mountain. He had hiked up 2150 feet in hopes of easing the tension in his body. His past haunted him, and his future terrified him. His thoughts turned to the horrid experiences he had in Lebanon. A few weeks after Ali had been captured and completed the first phase of terrorist training, he was sent out on a recruiting trip. When they arrived in his former village, Ali saw his friend, Alex, refuse to give in to the demands of the leader Aresh and dragged to a truck by the ISIS fighters. They just threw him in the back of the truck with others and sped away. When they all arrived back at camp, Ali felt deep shame because he pretended not to know Alex as Ali marched with the fighters past the new recruits. Ali was trying to protect himself from discovery.

There was no way Ali could protest Alex's capture, or Ali would face Aresh's anger and punishment. He had been captured weeks before Alex and was trying to keep a low profile, staying silent, compliant, and hoping that he wouldn't be brainwashed and forced to agree with Aresh's group of terrorists. Ali feared that he might not have the strength to resist becoming a terrorist.

Alex had always been the strong one in our friendship. Alex had tried to recruit me to join Omar and him in the new resistance groups some of our friends were forming, but I was too scared of repercussions or capture so I refused to join. When Omar worked in the Resistance, he was almost captured. He managed to escape just before I was captured several days after Alex's plea again for me to join the Resistance. ISIS tried to make me give up information about the resistance group's activities and their networks, but I firmly denied any knowledge. Playing dumb was preferable to giving in to Aresh's demands. I needed to avoid contact with Alex at all costs. The leaders needed to have no knowledge of our acquaintance. Both our lives depended on this. I knew if I even looked at Alex, I might give myself away.

Several days later, when Ali came back to camp after a training session on shooting rifles, Alex was gone from camp, and no one seemed to know where he had gone or even if Alex was still alive. Ali discreetly questioned anyone who might know of Alex's fate to no avail. Alex had disappeared, and Ali had no clue how.

If only I knew what happened to Alex. Was he killed for refusing Aresh, or did he finally give into him? Did he join the ISIS cause and lie about agreeing with their philosophies, or was he working undercover as a resistance fighter like Omar and trying to save his village and his family?

Yesterday, Omar Habbib had reached out to Ali and invited him to lunch at Sadie's restaurant. Ali pondered why the interest in him. He had to go because he didn't want anyone to get suspicious of his activities. He agreed to lunch because he sure could use a good meal.

Ali got up, brushed the leaves and twigs from his pants, and despondently headed out of the forest and into town to Sweet Indulgences for a hearty meal, which he desperately needed, and an interrogation, which he did not need.

Chapter 15

Uncertain Futures

After the band competition performance Saturday morning, the band members lined up at the buffet set up by the band parents in the parking lot. The hungry teens gobbled up cheeseburgers, fries, and potato salad topped off with ice cream for dessert.

"What will I do without my weekly walk to the ice cream shop for cones if I go off to college?" said Asher.

Mike was startled. "What do you mean if you go off to college? Where would you go? Do you have plans I don't know about? I thought you were going to junior college right here in Pittman."

"You know we all need to start thinking about what we are going to do after we graduate in June," said Asher. "I've been checking out colleges online in the northeast to see what they offer, and if I can find a match for my interests."

Mike, Billy. and Asher grabbed a seat at one of the picnic tables and looked seriously at each other.

"I feel like we need more time," said Mike. "With all that went on with the kidnapping of Billy, my dad's involvement, and then his going to prison, I feel like I'm being rushed into my future with no hand to guide me."

"Well, at least it will be your own choice. My mom

is laying a guilt trip on me because she wants me to follow in my dad's footsteps and go to the University of Kentucky. Even Matt Clare is pushing me. When he was here, he sat me down and tried to regale me with tales of how wonderful UK is from its great basketball team to their excellent gifted studies programs. I didn't have the nerve to tell him that I had no intention of going south again.

"My home now is here, where I can ski and follow my passion for music. What better place for music than here in the Berkshires where you can decide to play any instrument and immediately find a ready teacher of superior quality to teach you. There's a great music school affiliated with Princeton University that looks promising.

Asher continued. "I remember being here one summer when I was seven, and my dad took me to Tanglewood. They had a kid's day, and after you tried out the many instruments displayed, they offered lessons on any instrument you preferred. I decided on the violin. I then went five days a week for lessons, and after two weeks, we performed in Lennon's City Park on a big stage decorated with flowers. I was introduced by the master of ceremonies, stepped in front of an audience of about fifty people all sitting on blankets, clapping, and swinging to the music. I bowed, played my solo to ringing applause, then joined the other musicians in a combo set of bouncy tunes. I was hooked on music from that day on.

"The one thing that I relied on when my mom decided to settle here after Dad's death was that I would pursue a music career. I hate to disappoint my mom and Matt Clare, but I need to find a direction to a career right here. And they're not going to be too thrilled with that decision."

"That must be hard," Billy said. "You need to research a path either to a good college with a music curriculum or a music school focused on different types of music. If you find a couple of good choices, you might be able to convince your mom, but we'd better all get a move on. Early admission deadlines are in November for most colleges."

"What about you, Billy? What's your dream?" asked Mike.

"I'm pretty well set. Using my Aunt Dehlia's inheritance to buy into the partnership with Wayne in the motorcycle sales shop, and the repair shop was a wise step for me. I discovered I have a skill for repairing bikes and a talent for sales. What I'm lacking is the knowledge of the business side of everything, advertising, bookkeeping, taxes, etc. I found a two-year business college in Albany only an hour away that I can commute to two or three times a week for classes toward a business degree. I've applied for admission. Classes begin in the early fall, and Wayne is glad to cover for me when I have classes, if he keeps his word."

"I'm surprised this is the first we're hearing about this decision," said Asher.

"You have to admit we've all been pretty busy and haven't had much time to talk," said Billy.

"Yeah," said Mike, "some days all I want to think about is band, and sitting by one of the lakes watching the boats go by and, of course, watching the girls go by in the village square. I just can't seem to focus on school or career or anything beyond the day-by-day things. I'm so grateful to your mom, Asher, for letting me live with you all. Maybe I'll become a policeman and join forces with the super sleuths and Sheriff Houtman and help him accuse the right suspects of crimes."

"Would you really want to go into law enforcement? What kind of training would you need?" asked Billy.

"I have no clue. It's just a fantasy."

"Maybe not. You'd make a great policeman. You're smart, compassionate, and you've seen both sides of the law," said Asher. "Why don't you talk to Sheriff Houtman or Deputy Murphy about what kind of training you would need?"

"I'll think about it. I think I might need to move to another city after I graduate if my dad gets out of jail. I don't want to be in the same town as him."

"What about taking over your dad's bowling alley," Billy said, "or setting up another kind of business? We need another real estate agency since Ferguson went to jail. You seem to have a head for business. You were able to save your dad from bankruptcy because you have a knack for figures. How does a businessman's life sound to you? Then you could join Asher's mom, and Wayne and me in the Farley Square Business Association."

"I don't know. My dad suggested having Mr. H take over Ten Pins until he returns from prison. I think Mr. H would make a good caretaker of the bowling alley, and I don't think I want to be around town when my dad returns."

"I have another idea. You could work with Mr. Clare setting up the Children's Theater," suggested

Asher.

"You guys are sure full of ideas for my life, and they all involve my staying here. Hear me. I don't want to stay in Pittman. I think I'll wait until you decide, Asher. If you and Billy are going to be hanging around here, I might reconsider. Otherwise, I'm out of here. Maybe I'll join the FBI. They were recruiting the top students at school the other day. But right now, I'm getting another ice cream cone. This has been way too much thinking for me for one day."

"Then we need to set a meeting time again soon to talk about our future. Whatever we decide, we will need each other's support," said Billy.

"Okay, Sunday at Lennon City Park. Bring breakfast and blankets, and we plot our future destinies, or not. We could just stuff ourselves with donuts." Mike laughed.

Chapter 16

Tanglewood Sniper

The boys did not go to Lennon City Park on Sunday, but, instead, decided to spend the afternoon on the sprawling lawn at Tanglewood because the Boston Symphony was doing their last concert of the season, and the music was synchronized with a showing of a film. Since Mike and Asher enjoyed all the Tanglewood concerts, they convinced Billy to attend. They said, "Come on, Billy, if we have time, we will continue discussing our future plans."

The boys set out blankets, coolers, and a picnic basket filled with snacks and sandwiches, and then settled back in anticipation of a great experience. The sun was shining, which took the edge off the chill that was creeping in. The beautiful mature trees with multi-colored leaves provided a compliment to the luscious green grass of the lawn area.

I also attended the concert and was so proud of our local population. Sadie, Cameron, and I set out our chairs, blankets, and picnic baskets near the middle of the lawn in front of the stage. Cameron had his tape recorder and yellow reporter's pad ready to analyze the small-town scene. Andy was wandering around taking pictures as kids ran up to him and tried to get him to snap their pictures as they made funny faces and performed bizarre antics for the camera. I didn't see the sheriff, who would certainly be upset to see Cameron sitting with Sadie. Hopefully, he is on duty away from the concert.

I looked around and spotted Mr. Habbib with Ali and Ahmram, sitting near the back of the crowd. I was so glad that Mr. H had decided to open his house to Ali. The relationship was developing well. Mr. Habbib was helping Ali connect with shopkeepers to try to find a job. Meanwhile, Ali was helping Mr. Habbib with Ahmram's care. Ali had found a used car to buy so he now could seek out jobs in nearby towns. He has several prospects for jobs and is just waiting for final confirmation. His immigration status is causing a delay in his hiring process. Mr. Habbib and I are not sure what his immigration status is, and though Sadie and Omar are willing to vouch for his character because he was their friend, Sadie still hasn't a clue how he arrived here, or why he came to Pittman.

I also spotted Lola in a group with Andy and Deputy Murphy. *I'd like to be a fly on the wall to listen in on that conversation.* She looked so pretty, dressed in a pretty sunhat and colorful shorts with a yellow cotton blouse. She also had a beautiful wool shawl for after the sun set. I noticed a bouquet on her blanket. Three guesses who they were from. Ah, to be young again.

The concert was wonderful. Scenes from a film played on large screens, and the music played by the Boston Symphony Orchestra synchronized with each scene. Everyone gave the orchestra a standing ovation at intermission. The audience then brought out their picnics and wandered around to stretch their legs and buy ice cream and snacks before the second half of the performance.

About ten minutes into the twenty-minute intermission, a strange noise rang out that startled everyone. We all started looking around, seeking the source of the noise that sounded like a loud gunshot. Asher and Billy returning, holding ice cream cones, were shocked to see a black rifle had been tossed across their blanket. Asher reached out to pick it up and examine it when Billy yelled at him, "Don't touch that gun, Asher." Unfortunately, the damage was done. Asher had already picked up the rifle to examine it.

The crowd heard Billy shout and saw Asher holding the rifle. "Stop him," yelled the crowd near Asher. "Police, police, the shooter."

Deputy Murphy and the Tanglewood security guards ran toward Asher, yelling, "Drop that gun now." Asher froze. The security guards pulled out guns and handcuffs and aimed the guns at him. He was so surprised, he couldn't move. He just stood there and stared. One of the guards tackled Asher, and the other secured the rifle and handcuffed him. Deputy Murphy just looked on in disbelief.

Murphy said to the Chief of Security, "This has to be a mistake. I know this kid, and he wouldn't try to kill anyone. Was anyone hurt when the rifle was fired? Do we know what direction the bullet came from?"

By then, Sadie and I realized what was happening and ran to the boys' blanket. "Stop. I'm the boy's mother. Unhandcuff my son."

Murphy had to hold me back. "Easy, Robin. Let me handle this. We'll get it all sorted out. I know Asher wouldn't try to assassinate anyone. Let me calm everyone down, then we'll get to the bottom of this."

Murphy grabbed the head of security and said, "You need to send all of your officers to scour the park for the actual assassin. Obviously, he or she missed their target, tossed the gun, and escaped. I'll call Sheriff Houtman to help us figure this out. Time is of the essence. Leave Asher in the custody of his mother and her friend while we all hunt for who did this and determine who was the target."

The Chief of Security agreed with Deputy Murphy's suggestion, but he warned Sadie and me not to leave. Poor Asher. I don't know if he was more afraid of being arrested or more embarrassed because the whole audience saw him in handcuffs.

Sadie said to Asher, "Why did you pick up the rifle?"

"I wasn't thinking of anything but making sure the gunman couldn't grab the gun and start shooting at more people. I guess that was pretty stupid."

I asked my shaking son, "Did you see anyone drop the gun or run past your blanket?"

"No, everything happened so fast. Billy and I were just coming back from the ice cream stand and saw the rifle on our blanket. I dropped my ice cream and grabbed the gun just as Billy shouted not to touch it."

"I know many people were moving around. Did anyone see anything suspicious, or anyone who wasn't where they should be before the shooting?" asked Deputy Murphy.

Sadie said she glanced over at Mr. Habbib's blanket to see if Ahmram was having a good time and noticed that Ali was gone right before the shooting.

"Cameron Coldren went to get hot coffee for all of us, so he also was out and about during the time of the shooting," I said. "I also glanced over to see how Lola was enjoying the concert and noticed that she was seated all alone. That means the photographer was missing, but he could have been taking photographs. You should ask Andy if you can view any photos he took in case he inadvertently caught the assassin on film."

"Good idea."

When the sheriff arrived, he questioned all the security guards and Deputy Murphy, then he turned to Asher and said, "Young man, I'm taking you to the station, away from all these gawking people for questioning. Come with me to my patrol car."

Asher looked around at the crowd, dropped his head, and said, "Okay, sheriff."

I started to protest that he couldn't just take Asher without an adult or lawyer present.

"Calm down, Robin, you can meet us at the station with all the lawyers you want, but I'm just trying to spare Asher more embarrassment. Murphy, while I'm gone, be sure to question all who were in the vicinity of Asher's blanket and the area that the bullet came from. Like Robin suggested, check out Andy's photos, then meet me back at the office. Chief, I will keep you informed unless you want to accompany me."

"Sheriff, I'll leave that to you right now. I think my time will be better spent trying to determine where the shot came from, and who was the intended victim," said the chief of security.

Deputy Murphy made a loudspeaker announcement to the crowd. "A gunshot has been fired. If you saw the gun being shot or heard where the shot came from, please give me or one of the security guards your name, address, and phone number as you exit the park. They will call or email each attendee and question each of you. If any of you have any relative information, call the police station when you are safely out of the park. For now, do not panic, just go home. The concert has been canceled. The management says you can get a refund or voucher for a concert next summer if you mail in your ticket stub or email a picture of the stub to the box office. Please leave the park quickly. Drive carefully since a lot of cars will be leaving at once."

The sheriff started to lead Asher to his patrol car. I was to meet him at the police station since he had to have a responsible adult present for the interrogation.

Chapter 17

Vengeful Mom

Sadie, Lola, and I packed up our picnic gear. As we exited Tanglewood's parking lot, we got caught in a huge traffic jam.

As we left, the security guards were searching the grounds for any clues about the assassin, grateful that he or she had failed to kill anyone. When we cleared the traffic jam, Sadie dropped me off at the sheriff's office. Just before she left, I asked her to assemble the Super Sleuths. I told her I would join them at Sweet Indulgences after getting Asher settled at home.

After Sadie left, I burst into the station in a huff. "Sheriff, I demand you release Asher this minute," I raged at the incompetent man.

"Now, Robin, calm down. All the evidence points to Asher as the shooter. His fingerprints are on the rifle. Witnesses saw him holding the gun. He claimed they had been buying ice cream for the three boys, but only one cone was dropped at the scene. Where were the other two cones?" Sheriff Houtman continued, "Dropping his cone could have been a detraction. Also, you can't deny the evidence of the fingerprints on the rifle."

"Well, of course his fingerprints were on the gun. He picked it up to protect others. As for the ice cream

94

cones, he could have given Mike his cone as he walked through the park and Billy was right behind him, so he would have his cone. The boys were wandering around. Have you asked Mike if Asher gave him his cone?"

Ignoring me, the sheriff continued, "Murphy told me that they found an imprint of a size eight shoe by the gate where the shooter probably exited."

Robin said, "Asher wears a size ten since he's tall for his age, just like his dad."

"Does Asher own a rifle?" asked Mark Houtman.

"Well of course he does, as do most kids from this area. It's common for kids to embark on hunting trips in the Spring to shoot the excess deer population, but mostly they shoot rabbits and wild turkeys. Does it prove him a killer just because he goes hunting? Because a person, particularly from this area of Massachusetts, owns a gun, proves nothing. Plus, the rifle on the blanket looked entirely different from the gun owned by Asher. Sheriff, your reasoning is faulty. Sadie owns a gun. Does that make her an assassin? No, she owns a gun to protect herself from any ISIS fighter set for revenge. She will protect herself, her friends, and her family, but that doesn't make her a mad killer.

"While you are interrogating others, may I take Asher home now?" I asked the sheriff in a desperately forced, calm voice.

"Robin, I understand your protectiveness of Asher, but until proven otherwise, Asher stays here in jail as my main suspect. Even if he isn't the shooter, he's safer here in the jail, particularly if there is a shooter who is still out there, and who might have seen Asher pick up the gun. Go home, and we'll talk tomorrow. Come here about noon."

"I will, and I will bring a lawyer if you still mistakenly insist on charging my son as an assassin. Sometimes, sheriff, you exasperate me. You are so stubborn. Open your eyes and lose the pompous attitude before you let the real shooter get away." I wanted to hug Asher before I left, but he was so embarrassed, he turned away from me and the sheriff took him back to his cell. So instead, I turned and stomped out of the station, hitting my hands with my fists, wishing I were hitting that stubborn man.

Chapter 18

The Super Sleuths Must Intervene Again

When Sadie dropped Robin at the police station, she said, "Don't worry, Robin, we'll solve this. I'll go right to the restaurant and text Lola, Mike, and Billy to meet us there. Once again, the Super Sleuths need to solve a mystery.

After leaving the jail, I joined the Super Sleuths at Sweet Indulgence. Once again, our band of amateur sleuths must prove the innocence of someone they love, since the inept sheriff believes the wrong person is the perpetrator of a crime.

"When will he ever learn to listen to reason?" I said to Sadie.

I then said to the Super Sleuths, "Thank you so much for coming to help us solve another mystery. This time Sheriff Houtman is convinced Asher was the shooter, but, hopefully, the sheriff isn't dumb enough to go down that road again. He has never trusted Billy, even though we proved that he had nothing to do with the last murder that happened last year in Pittman. He grudgingly acknowledged that Billy was innocent, but nothing could convince him to trust Billy. Now, he refuses to release Asher, and he will need to sleep at the jail tonight. Sheriff Houtman refused to listen to my reasoning and my pleas to release the poor kid. Asher is a nervous young man."

Sadie provided snacks as we all sat down to begin investigating. As we ate, we listed questions, ideas, and suspicions. I summarized what had happened at the jail.

Lola began by telling everyone what she learned from Deputy Murphy before she left Tanglewood. "Robert Murphy told me he went with the security police to try to determine where the rifle shot originated. He told me they found a crushed bush at gate C, so they are assuming that's where the shooter either came into the park or hastily exited after failing to hit his or her target. They found a shoeprint about size eight that looked to be a man's shoe."

"If they think the shooter exited the park via exit C, it couldn't have been Asher because he was still in the park picking up the dropped rifle on his blanket," said Mike.

"Good point," we all echoed.

"Did anyone see or hear anything suspicious?" I asked.

"I heard a popping sound and a swish," said Billy.

"Some of the people questioned as they were exiting the park said they thought the sound was just a drummer warming up on stage," said Lola.

"Does anyone know which direction the shot came from or how many shots were fired?" asked Lola.

"I heard two pops, but it was so fast, I can't be sure from which direction they came," said Billy.

Lola said, "Deputy Murphy also told me they think the shots were fired from the back of the grassy seating area, and the park security agents are combing the woods facing the grassy area where everyone sat. They also are searching the area looking for spent cartridges, but haven't yet found anything, and it's getting dark, so they will have to resume the search tomorrow."

"Wouldn't that rule out Asher as a suspect since he came from the ice cream stand which is in front, beside the stage?" asked Mike.

"You would think that would exonerate him, but the sheriff thinks Asher lied about heading right from the ice cream stand to his picnic area, and he doesn't trust Billy's word. Mike, when did Asher give you your ice cream cone?"

"Right when he got it from the ice cream stand and when he saw me talking to some of the band kids."

"Mr. Habbib is contacting his brother, who is a lawyer in Great Barrington, to see if he can get Asher bailed out or released to Robin's custody," said Sadie. "Asher has no prior convictions for any crime so he should be able to get him out of jail, especially after he points out the directional evidence of the bullet to the sheriff."

"Do the investigators know who was targeted by the assassin?" asked Mike.

"Not yet," said Lola.

"Maybe our first chore should be making a list of possible targets and motives for the shooter," I said.

"Okay." Efficient Lola had a large chart and marker to record our findings.

Targets:

Billy, Asher, Sadie, someone on stage, a security guard, Deputy Murphy, Andy, Cameron

Motives/Evidence:

—The rifle was found on Billy and Asher's picnic blanket while the boys were absent during intermission.

—Sadie might be targeted by an ISIS member

seeking revenge because of her sympathy for the Resistance fighters in Lebanon.

—Someone may have a grudge against law enforcement and may be targeting one of the security guards or Deputy Murphy,

—Anyone on stage or in the audience might be targeted by someone who hates them.

—Andy was wandering around taking pictures. Could one of Andy's photos have offended someone?

—Cameron was at our picnic area, which was in the path of the shot. Could someone be angry because of a story he has reported?

We all looked at the list.

"I think we can rule out Omar Habbib, Ali, and Ahmram as targets because their picnic area was back near the trees. Since the shot came from the back area, the shooter would have to be a very bad shot to miss them," Lola said.

Lola pulled down another poster sheet of paper. "Let's make a list of the possible shooters. If we can narrow down a list of suspected shooters, we should be able to show Sheriff Houtman that others had a motive besides Asher."

"Good idea," I said. "This entire process is taking too much time. Meanwhile, I haven't yet heard from Samuel Habbib, our lawyer. I don't even know if he will take on Asher's case. I am worried that Asher is just sitting in that jail feeling humiliated and scared. We need to contact Samuel Habbib and see if he has talked to the sheriff about releasing Asher, or if he hasn't, we need to ask if he is free at noon tomorrow to accompany me to the sheriff's office."

"You're right, Robin. Lola, let's see if we can

come to some conclusions to present to the sheriff," said Sadie.

"Okay, let's get our list of possible shooters down first, then we will justify our conclusions to present to Sheriff Wrong. Mike, can you man the Bookworm shop, or I can ask Edna Mae? Lola, could you handle Sadie's restaurant since you are familiar with most of the food offered and know most of her customers?"

"Sure, Robin, I'll practice some of my improv ideas on the customers."

Mike said, "Why don't you ask Edna Mae to handle the sales at your bookstore? I'd like to do some snooping on my own."

"Good idea. I'm sure Edna Mae will agree to step in," I said.

Lola got out another sheet of the chart and started to mark it up.

Possible Shooters and Why

—Ali- According to Mr. Habbib, Ali had left their picnic area before the shooting, and no one knows where he went. Also, we don't know much about his activities for the past few years because he changes the subject whenever we ask about his past.

—Mr. Habbib—He says he took Ahmram to the play area, but does anyone know how long he stayed there? Could he want revenge on anyone who harassed him when he came to town? He did take his son to the play area, but Aunt Florence told Sadie that she and some of the older ladies offered to watch Ahmram play while Mr. Habbib went for refreshments.

—Billy or Asher–They had each vacated their picnic area and vouched for each other. Billy says he and Asher went for ice cream and then returned to the blanket at about the same time. Then Billy saw Asher pick up the gun that was already lying on the blanket. If that is true, it would eliminate Asher and Billy. However, the sheriff is convinced that Billy or Asher, or both are lying.

—Stranger–A tourist with a grudge against someone may want to destroy the reputation of our town as a peaceful tourist destination.

—Mr. Nelson from the Pet Shop–He seems angry with the entire world.

—Milo–He might be out to kill his dad because of his abuse. Does anyone know where Nelson and Milo were seated?

Lola said, "I saw them make a late entrance into the park. The music had already begun, but I didn't see where they sat."

—Cameron–Do we know if he has a history of violence? Does he have any enemies he might want to eliminate? We don't know why he chose our town for his video documentary. Could that be a cover for his animosity toward someone in Pittman?

We all looked over the list. I said, "I think we can rule out Mr. Habbib as the shooter. He seems like a devoted father, and just recently he was counseling Ali. He convinced Ali not to live in the Pittman Forest, but rather to move in with him and Ahmram."

The others agreed to eliminate him as the suspected shooter, but Billy asked, "Could he be the intended target? Does anyone know who hates him enough to want him dead?"

We all pondered this idea.

Lola said, "There are several locals who often voice their displeasure at the foreigners descending on our small town. Just last week, a busload of thirty illegal immigrants from the border in Arizona were offloaded in a village north of here. No one in authority there knew what to do with them since no one alerted law enforcement that they were coming. Many locals appeared outside the police station carrying signs that said, 'Go Home Now.' I think these busloads have been offloaded in several towns in the Berkshires and other New England towns."

I said, "I've heard some locals insult Mr. Habbib and harass his son in the carpool lane at school. He's here legally because when he fled from the violence in his village, his brother stepped in to sponsor him and immediately had one of the lawyers in his firm get permission to offer Omar asylum because if he went back to Lebanon, he would be killed. When the lawyer pointed out that Omar's wife died while in the refugee camp, his refugee status was granted."

Billy said, "You all know what Sadie went through when she first arrived legally, sponsored by her aunt. Remember the day they vandalized the restaurant? One of those men is now dead, but I'm sure there are still some who harbor a deep prejudice even though she's been here for four years."

"The sheriff needs to question Omar Habbib," I said, "to see who has threatened him since he came to town. He also needs to ask Ali if anyone has threatened him."

"We will add Mr. Habbib to the victim's list," Lola said. "Let's take him off the shooter list. Okay, now it's time to review our lists and gather our thoughts. Write down on a piece of paper:

—Who do you think is the shooter?

—Who do you think was the intended victim?

—Who do you think has a motive for the intended assassination?"

After we all voted, Lola collected and collated the votes, then she announced the results:

"Victim–Sadie, a security guard, or Cameron

Shooter–Mr. Nelson, Ali, or a stranger wanting to destroy our town's reputation, or someone who hates illegal immigrants."

I said, "Now, write down the reasons Sheriff Houtman should release Asher. If our lawyer has not gotten Asher released, we will ask him to be present tomorrow at the meeting also. Sadie and I will go to the meeting at noon, settle the release of Asher, and we will give Sheriff Houtman the Super Sleuths' findings. We'll let you all know what happens. Meanwhile, keep your eyes and ears open to anything out of the ordinary."

Chapter 19

Release Asher Now

Sadie and I met with Sheriff Houtman and Deputy Murphy at noon the next day after Asher had spent the night in jail. Mr. Omar Habbib's lawyer brother, Samuel, went with us. Samuel Habbib told us that he had called the sheriff the night before, and demanded Asher be released right then, but the stubborn sheriff refused.

"This is my son you are holding as prisoner," I said. I was raging mad.

"Now calm down, Robin," the sheriff said. "Let me see the findings of your Super Sleuths." The sheriff reviewed our lists of possible shooting victims and motives. He then said, "Now that you have a substantial amount of evidence and alternative shooters as suspects, we'll check it out."

Samuel Habbib said, "Sheriff, you should see now that there are many possibilities for the shooter, and the case against Asher shows that he is the weakest suspect, and his guilt is negated because of the strong evidence."

When Mr. Samuel Habbib continued to insist that the case against Asher must be dismissed, Deputy Murphy interrupted and said, "I feel the security guards have exonerated Asher with their evidence of the directional path of the bullet and where the shooter would have had to be standing to shoot it on that path."

Sheriff Houtman said, "But the further testimony of witnesses proves that Asher isn't this calm kid you are claiming. He has a temper. I need time to question Asher's friends. I asked Asher if he had any enemies. He denied it.

"But that isn't what Deputy Murphy found out from questioning some of his classmates at Tanglewood. I have set up a time today to question those students myself. After I question them, I will fill you in on what I find, but I will need to keep Asher here to get his reaction to the kids' statements. After that, I will consider releasing Asher into your custody, Robin. I will call you soon, Mr. Habbib."

Samuel Habbib and I left the station and went to Sweet Indulgences to wait for the sheriff's call. Sadie tried to calm me down, but nothing would calm me until Asher was safely at home with me. "My respect for the sheriff is about zero right now. I know you think he is wonderful, Sadie, but I can't agree with that. He is so stubborn."

After questioning witnesses at Tanglewood, the Chief of Security told three classmates of Ashers to get their parents and report to the jailhouse to be questioned by the sheriff. When the three teenage boys arrived at the jailhouse with their parents, Sheriff Houtman interviewed each boy separately. Their stories were identical.

"I heard that you had an argument with Asher that made him very angry. Can you tell me what that was all about?" asked the sheriff.

They each told the sheriff that Asher was an avid fan of the music at the concert, and he had been trying to get them to sell him their collection of rare figurines associated with them. They refused to sell, and Asher was trying to scare them into selling by yelling at them.

When the boys left the station, Sheriff Houtman phoned Robin's lawyer. He related the teenagers' testimony to the lawyer while Samuel had Robin on speakerphone. The sheriff explained, "The boys accused Asher of calling them a bunch of rich snobs, so they yelled back at Asher hurling insults at him about being a fatherless kid who wanted to own figurines because they reminded him of the toys he had that his dad gave him as a child. Other witnesses told Deputy Murphy that they heard the teenagers call Asher a 'wimp.'"

Sheriff Houtman, to his credit, was no fool. "Mind you, I think there is a possibility that Asher is still guilty of shooting the rifle, but I am willing to release Asher into his mother's custody with the caution that he is not to leave town. I will hold you, Mr. Habbib, as their lawyer, and Robin accountable, to make sure Asher doesn't leave town and is available for further questioning."

"Thank you, sheriff. We agree to your terms, and we will be right there to take Asher home."

Mr. Samuel Habbib handed Asher over to my custody. When we left the station, Asher threw himself into my arms, sobbing. I let him cry, then said, "Let's all go to Sweet Indulgences and have a sundae to assuage your trauma from spending time in jail."

Relieved, they all agreed. I was glad Samuel Habbib joined us because we needed to thank him and ask him where to go from here. We also needed to find out what he thought about his brother, Omar, being the victim or even perhaps the shooter. I wasn't sure how much the two brothers had kept in touch, but surely with Omar now in the Berkshires, the two brothers will catch up on the past and be looking forward to sharing their futures as Omar gets settled in Pittman.

When we left, Sheriff Houtman got an anonymous phone call complaining that Omar Habbib was harboring a criminal, an illegal immigrant. The sheriff confronted Mr. Habbib when he saw him on his way to Sweet Indulgences. "Mr. Habbib, you know nothing about this young man. He could be up to no good."

Omar protested. "Sadie and I knew Ali in Lebanon, and his family lived next door to my mom and dad. He was also best friends with Alex, Sadie's brother. We all ran around together getting into all kinds of mischief, but we also did a lot of good in the neighborhood. If we saw a need, we helped out."

The sheriff said, "But what you and Sadie aren't considering is his present-day connections. Is he still a good kid, or has all the turmoil in his village turned him into a thug? I suspect that Sadie suggested this housing solution, and she is too trusting."

"Actually, no. I suggested it," said Omar Habbib.

"What do you know about any of Ali's current activities? For instance, how did he get into the country, and why did he come to an obscure town like Pittman? I'm just trying to protect you and Sadie."

When Sheriff Houtman confronted Sadie later that day, he expected her to explain why she was involved in Mr. Habbib's harboring an undocumented immigrant, but she screamed at Sheriff Houtman. "I am perfectly able to make my own judgements and decisions. I am an independent woman and don't need you, Mark Houtman, protecting me and doubting my abilities. I am tired of you and your patronizing ways with women."

Chapter 20

Deputy Murphy Weighs In

The sheriff headed into his office shaking his head. "I'll never understand women."

Sheriff Houtman and Deputy Murphy spent the morning on paperwork and researching Cameron. They bounced different ideas back and forth about the theft of the instruments at the school, the money stolen at Jiminy Peak, and now the assassination attempt at Tanglewood. They decided the only possible tie between these crimes would be if it was an amateur, probably a teenager, someone from the band, or from the town.

About three-o-clock, the sheriff stretched and said, "I'm going over to Sweet Indulgences for a late lunch. Do you want me to bring you back a sandwich or muffin, Murphy?"

"Oh no, Mark, I brought my own sandwich, a delicious peanut butter and jelly on white bread. How could I possibly eat a homemade chicken salad sandwich or blueberry muffin instead of peanut butter and jelly."

"Well, okay, if you prefer that."

"Mark, I'm being sarcastic. You haven't a clue. What kind of detective are you?"

Mark laughed. "Not a particularly good one, I

guess, as Robin and Sadie often accuse. Nuances have never been my strong point. I'll bring you a sandwich and a muffin."

Sheriff Houtman walked to Sweet Indulgences. As he passed the bike shop, he looked through the window and spotted Cameron with Billy and Wayne. Cameron was writing on his notepad as he was interviewing the young men. *Maybe I'm wrong about Cameron. Maybe he is a legitimate journalist and is doing his preparations for this video documentary series. I'll be glad when he finally leaves town.*

When Mark entered Sweet Indulgences, he looked around for Sadie, hoping she could sit with him and talk for a while. Since Cameron came to town, she had been distracted by all the hoopla surrounding the show and hadn't had much time for him. He missed their almost daily chats, but luck wasn't with him. One of the waitresses had called in sick, and Sadie was running between the kitchen making the savory treats and helping the other waitress deliver orders and work the cash register. She barely had time to wave at him.

Mark had hoped Sadie would agree with his suspicion of Nelson's son, Milo, for stealing the band instruments and the money at Jiminy Peak and his suspicion of Asher as the shooter. He knew Sadie and Robin would rebel if he arrested another teenager after the debacle with Asher, but Milo had been seen after band practice looking into lockers in the band room and left with a large package stuffed into his oversized jacket. At Jiminy Peak, he was also seen taking his breaks from Nelson's Pet Shop booth and walking up and down the rows of rides and booths, constantly looking over his shoulder. Then at Tanglewood, Nelson and he came into the concert late and sat in the back where they would have had direct access to the area where the gunshot was fired. This suspicious behavior led to suspicion of Milo, and Mark didn't want the wrath of the Super Sleuths on him again for suspecting a teenager.

Disappointed that Sadie had no time to discuss his concerns, Mark headed back to the station to process the paperwork for Milo's possible arrest if they could find enough evidence to prove his guilt. He had to solve these crimes. The local community was getting restless. They weren't used to looking over their shoulders in fear of what was going to happen next.

On his walk back to the station, the sheriff looked in the window of Nelson's Pet Shop. Standing by the snake cages, Cameron and Nelson were having a heated discussion. Nelson was waving a small boa constrictor at Cameron as they were locked in a fierce argument. It certainly didn't look like an innocent interview with a shop owner for his videocast or an argument between strangers, but one between long-term adversaries. This was the second argument between the two men that Sheriff Houtman had witnessed. Cameron's face was livid as he pointed at Nelson, and Nelson looked mighty menacing flinging around that boa.

I wonder what is going on. I'm not a fan of Horatio Nelson because he's so opinionated and a bully, but it looks like Horatio might be on the losing end of this argument despite the boa he holds.

The parrot, Feathers, was squawking and jumping up and down in his cage. What a sight! Sheriff Houtman knocked on the store window and shouted, "Is everything okay?" The men stopped abruptly and nodded yes, so the sheriff continued back to the office.

At the station, as Deputy Murphy was eating his sandwich, Sheriff Houtman said to him, "Murphy, we need to do some clandestine surveillance of this journalist. I haven't found out much about him as I researched. Coldren seems to have a conflict with Nelson. There's plenty of info on Coldren's last three years as a podcaster and the producer of many video documentaries, but I can't find out much about his professional or personal life before that, which seems suspicious. Nelson is also relatively new to town; he's only owned the Pet Shop for one year, and I'm not sure where he lived and worked before now. I'm going to follow Cameron Coldren tomorrow, then I'd like you to shadow him on Monday. I know it's your day off, but this needs to be done right away."

Deputy Murphy stared at the sheriff. "No," Murphy said.

"What did you say?"

"I said, 'no.' It's my day off, and I have a life outside of this job, a life where people know my name and care about me as a person. Mark, what do you know about me? Do you ever ask about the things I like or do? Do you even know my first name?"

"Well of course I do. What is this nonsense? I have worked with you every day for four years."

"Mark, you call me Deputy Murphy or just plain Murphy. You never call me by my first name. What is it?"

"Darn it, Murphy. I forget, okay? I forget your first name. I guess I'm not only a bad detective who doesn't detect sarcasm, but also a poor boss who forgets names. What, are you going to quit because I can't recall your first name?"

"No, I'm not quitting, but I won't be putting in any overtime either."

With that said, Murphy went outside to cool down, and Mark Houtman paced the room, lost in thought. He rebuked himself. *I need to be more attentive to Murphy's needs. He's right. He's also young, and I think, according to the local florist, he has a crush on a young lady, and blast it, I don't even know who. I must make some time to talk to my deputy and be more aware of his needs.*

Mark had no excuse. He realized he was still in grieving mode for his wife and had trouble letting other people into his life. Even with Sadie, he found himself reserved and sometimes even aloof, though he found her fascinating. *I need to reform and soon, or I will lose my loyal employee and my enticing friend.*

Chapter 21

Putting Tradition Aside

Sadie announced at her last traditional Sunday barbeque that she thought we needed to think about making up a different menu or having a theme to get some variety into our lives.

"But, Sadie," protested Lola, "we love your traditional Lebanese food."

"Yes, we would miss it, especially the lamb dishes," said Sheriff Houtman and Mr. H. together."

"I think I speak for all the young people here," said Mike. "We would enjoy something different. Why don't we experiment with three Sundays a month, something new, and one day, traditional?"

"Good idea," said Asher and Billy,

"Okay, agreed. Let me know what and who is bringing food and set up a schedule," I told everyone.

"Robin, do you think we could do some improv? It might be fun. I could plan a trial improv for next Sunday. Let me know the menu and what the theme is ahead of time, and I will come up with something," said Lola.

Mr. H said, "I am going to miss the grape leaves and hummus, but I guess I'll go along with whatever everyone wants since I'm the newest member of this gourmet picnic group."

Sadie said, "The first change we are going to make is, we are going to have a matinee lunch on the third Sunday of this month because Lola will have finished her season at Shakespeare and Company. We'll celebrate her success."

"I've got an idea," said Billy. "Let us boys come up with the menu. Ali, that includes you and Ahmram. Okay?"

They all said, "We're in."

After dinner, the boys went to the sideyard and huddled together to come up with ideas. It was good to see the young people get excited about the changes.

When Ali went home that night with Mr. Habbib, he thought, *"Everyone here is accepting me as part of their extended family. This wasn't supposed to happen. How can I carry out my assignment now? I can't do it. I regret my decision. What can I do?*

****

Mike, Asher, and Billy were anxious to get together to talk again about their future plans. They decided to meet the next day since it was a school holiday, so there were no classes or band practice. At lunchtime, they met at Lennon City Park, but they found that the near future was a bit more pressing than their futures after graduation. They needed to pursue clues as to who the shooter was so they all felt safely exonerated from suspicion.

"I'm inclined to suspect Ali," said Billy. "Sadie keeps vouching for him. Did you all know Ali used to be friends with her older brother, Alex in Lebanon? I think she had a crush on Ali when she was a little girl. That might be why she keeps defending him."

"Wow," said Mike. "No one seems to know where

Ali was when the sniper shot and missed at Tanglewood."

After the discussion was going nowhere because no one had any hard evidence, Mike said, "On a lighter subject, is everyone planning to go to the Costume Ball at the high school on Halloween?"

Billy said, "This is the first time I've heard about it. I saw some posters in the halls, but I've been so busy that I didn't take the time to read them and think about it."

"No one should be that busy, Billy. You need to stop and have some fun. We're only teenagers once," said Mike.

"I know, but Wayne has been taking these mysterious three-or four-day trips. I often just find a closed sign on the door when I show up for work. I never know when he is going or when he will return. When Wayne returns, he always has cash that he gives me for expenses since I keep the books. I'm getting worried as well as tired from all the extra work."

"That seems strange," said Mike. "I hope he isn't into something shady or illegal."

"So do I," said Billy. Changing the subject, Billy said, "As you said, on a lighter subject. Are we supposed to bring dates?"

"Well," Mike said, "according to the lovely Karen Martin, my lab partner, some are going with dates, and some are going in groups, boys and girls, or just guys, or just girls. I asked Karen what she was doing, and she said that she wasn't sure yet. Some of the kids in the science class said they were creating some weird versions of Frankenstein and aliens for their costumes. Then they planned to stage an invasion at the dance. I volunteered to be the announcer of the invasion. I have an amplified mic and strobe lights to announce the aliens' entrance. I'm practicing my amplified voice of doom. Karen thinks it's a hysterical idea, so I convinced her to dress as an alien princess and come with me to the dance. Not sure if it's a real date, but it should be fun. What about you all? Any ideas? "

Billy said, "Your idea sounds like a blast. What if I decorate a motorcycle with blinking lights and lead in the alien invasion?"

"Great idea, but where does that leave me? I'm not exactly the invasion sort of guy, and I'm not exactly in a party mood with all that's happened to me over the last few days," said Asher.

"I've got it," said Mike. "You could dress as a professor, and Karen's cute friend, Mandy, could dress as a TV interviewer. After the invasion, when things have settled down, you and Mandy could go up on stage. We could put a spotlight on you, and you could pretend that Mandy is interviewing you about your knowledge of the existence of extraterrestrials. We might even be able to get Susie from the band to compose a wild dance tune for everyone to dance to just before the spotlight turns to the stage."

"Do you think we'll get in trouble for disrupting the dance? I've had enough trouble with authority," said Asher.

"Not if we get one of the teachers or chaperones involved. Let's feel out a few teachers that might be up for some fun," said Billy. "Text us if you find someone in authority to back us. Once this is a go, we can meet at my repair shop and practice."

"I don't know Karen and Mandy very well," said

Asher, "but I have had a secret crush on Susie since we've been in band. Let me ask her about composing the dance tune. Maybe I can even ask her to save time to dance with me."

"Why, Asher, you Casanova you."

Asher blushed and then passed out the donuts.

Switching back, Asher said, "Let's wait until we get a commitment from a teacher before we go overboard. Right now, let's think about our original ideas about our future after we graduate."

The boys all agreed and began to relish the sweetness of donuts. It was quiet for a while as they ate and turned inward to fantasies about dances, aliens, and their futures.

Mike came up with an idea as he bit into a chocolate cream donut. "I think Ms. White, our band director, would be willing to help us since most of us involved are in band. I'll call her right now."

Mike was elated. "She agreed to join us. She really was excited."

Asher said, "I'm glad that's settled. I hope you all don't think I'm a wimp for needing a teacher's approval, but I don't want to do anything that might get us in trouble right now."

Billy said, "We understand. It's a go. Aliens, get to work."

Chapter 22

Nightmares

When Billy got home, he was thinking about college or any future plans besides protecting himself from what he saw at Tanglewood. That night he woke from a nightmare, screaming.

Sadie ran into his room. "Billy, wake up. You were screaming. Did you have a nightmare?"

Billy just put his arms around Sadie and hugged her tightly and only let go when he fell asleep in her arms.

Sadie gently put him down to sleep and determined to share this happening with Robin the next day.

When Sadie told me on the phone the next morning, I was stumped. "Do you think the nightmare was about something from his past, like his kidnapping, or do you think it has something to do with the shooting at Tanglewood?"

"He's never had a nightmare since he's lived with me. You don't think Billy could have seen the shooter, do you? He was in the right place and saw Asher pick up the rifle."

"I don't know. We should tell Sheriff Houtman about this."

"I will," said Sadie. "He's stopping by for breakfast."

****

After several weeks of living with Mr. Habbib and Ahmram, Ali was astounded at his own reformation. Mr. H asked him to take Ahmram to the park to play because he was going to look at a property where he might be able to open a small grocery. Ali agreed but was reluctant.

At the park, Ali thought about how he was becoming fond of this young kid, and he wished he had a brother just like him. "Ali, Ali, catch me when I slide down on my stomach. I don't want to hit my head. Will you catch me, Ali?"

****

When Ahmram looks at me with those trusting eyes and his smile which spreads across his dimpled face, I feel like I'm melting. No one has looked at me in that way since Alex and I used to tease Sadie, and she would run up to me and hug me, knowing that I loved her. How can I possibly kill Sadie as Aresh has commissioned me to do? She is that little girl who looked up to me. Alex is my best friend. What was I thinking? Money and power, that's what I desired.

When Ali brought Ahmram home from the park, he went to his room to think.

Aresh ordered me to assassinate Sadie and Omar Habbib because they were former Resistance workers. In return, Aresh would pay all my expenses. He thought about Sadie. *I can't kill someone I know. Why do I have to be the one who assassinates Sadie and Omar? I won't do it. I tried at Tanglewood and deliberately missed. I thought about what Alex would say if he found out I was the one who killed his younger sister and our friend Omar. I'm going to be in big trouble with Aresh.*

What is Aresh's long-term plan for creating terror and for revenge killings?

What will Sadie think when she finds out the boy she loved like a brother in her youth, tried to kill her? I have nothing but respect for Omar Habbib. Why should I kill him? He's been so kind to me, and he's such a wonderful father. Omar reminds me of my father. Omar was always the most responsible one of our trio of friends.

Ali was having second thoughts. While in the heat of battle in Lebanon, being a hitman sounded like a good assignment. He would gain much money and prestige. He would become almost as legendary as Aresh. In effect, ISIS's brainwashing had been turning Ali into a loyal terrorist.

Ali thought back to that night when he arrived at the Boston airport hotel preparing for his job when a knock at the door frightened him. When he opened the door, a man dressed in a dark topcoat stepped into his room. Ali immediately disliked the man.

The sinister man said, "I am a friend of your friend, Aresh. I know about your assignment in Pittman. Here is all the equipment and paperwork you need. I've also included a suggested timeline and several sites that might be best to take out your targets.

"I too have someone in Pittman who needs to be eliminated. He is a partner who has betrayed me. I have a setup to launder money from my drug business, and this partner is supposed to launder that drug money for me. Lately, though, he has been skimming more and more money off the top and altering the books to disguise this treachery. I have decided to have him eliminated as an example to my other partners in this drug business. No one messes with me. They need to know that I will not put up with cheaters. Aresh suggested that you would be the right person for the job.

"I am willing to pay big money if you are successful. You will get half of the payment ahead of time and the other half when the deed is done. It won't be too difficult. I'll supply you with the details, and you decide how and when you will carry out this assignment. However, it is critical that you keep my involvement in this crime completely confidential. No one can know I am behind this hit. You are to keep all the details secret from everyone. If you betray me or implicate me in the killing, you will meet the same fate as your mark. I will give you until tomorrow morning to decide. I'll meet you here in your room at precisely eight." With that speech, the mystery man left, and Ali let out his breath and collapsed on the couch.

After flashing back to his commission to be an assassin, Ali made a decision that would affect his future. *I need money since Aresh is only paying my expenses to assassinate Sadie and Mr. H. If I choose to kill this drug lord's mark, I could use that money to hide away in some small town in the USA and leave the life of ISIS behind. Maybe I could even make a new life for myself.*

Now, however, if I don't kill the drug lord's mark, the drug lord will kill me. How did I ever agree to kill anyone? I need help to untangle this mess.

Chapter 23

Lola Reveals Her Plans to Robin

When I walked into my Bookworm Shop Tuesday morning, I found a strange sight. Lola was on the floor crawling around in a circle then flipping onto her back and flailing her legs in the air. Over and over, she repeated these weird antics.

Unaware of my entrance, Lola then began to sing a song, "Oh, the mighty turtle isn't so mighty anymore. He flips on his back and wishes he had a sack to hide in. Flip and hide; flip and hide; oh, Zack the Turtle, who loves to flip on his back."

I crept forward but stubbed my toe on a bookcase. Lola heard the sound and jumped to her feet, her face turning red with embarrassment.

"Lola, what on earth are you doing, and why are you singing that ridiculous song?"

"Now, Robin, I haven't lost my mind as you seem to think. I'm practicing an acting exercise that helps portray a character, the turtle, having difficulty with his life. He then conquers his difficulties by flipping his problems away and singing a song to celebrate."

"I'm sure you have a reason for this performance," I said.

"Um, I do. I have been meaning to discuss a project with you that involves acting, but I didn't want to disturb you when Matt was in town. Do you have time now, or can we set aside about an hour later today? I need your help and approval for a project leading to a new direction in my career."

"I didn't know you were looking for a new career, but okay, Lola. I have a book rep due in about a half hour; you have story hour, and I am hosting the Geezer Book Club at three. Asher and Mike have band practice so why don't we go to dinner at about six thirty at Sweet Indulgences, and you can give me all the details. Is this something you might want to share with Sadie? I can ask her to join us if you want. I think this is her night off while Aunt Florence runs the dinner shift."

"That would be great, and yes, I could also use Sadie's input. I would like her advice since I've already clued her in, but then she got busy, and we couldn't continue the conversation. I respect her meticulous way of handling the details of a business."

All day, Lola seemed distracted as she waited on many customers.

When the members of the Geezer Book Club came at three, the topic of discussion was a mystery book titled *Deception*. The discussion went off track almost immediately as Edna Mae filled in Bart O'Neal, Beth, and Marie about what happened at the Ski Fest Planning Meeting. They each agreed to help out with the rides at the Fest. I was relieved that they were ready to volunteer. Now all of the rides, food booths, and business booths were covered by volunteers.

"What do we know about this Cameron Coldren?" asked Bart, their resident researcher.

Edna said, "We know that he is supposedly a respected journalist from Boston who broadcasts a

Podcast each Friday on the radio and a video documentary series on BPR once a month. For the documentary, he is doing a feature on the way of life in smaller towns in the Berkshires," answered Edna.

"I assume then that he will be filming during the Fest?" asked Bart O'Neal.

Mr. Brump asked, "How long has Cameron Coldren been doing this documentary series?"

"I have no idea, but on Fridays, many locals and tourists gather at Sweet Indulgences to listen to the podcasts. I have also gone to the restaurant once a month to see Cameron Coldren, on his documentaries. He is dreamy, and we all enjoy looking at him," said Edna.

"I don't trust anyone with his good looks. See how he has already charmed Lola, Sadie, and even Edna Mae. I predict that trouble is coming," said Marie.

Neal said, "Let's not jump to conclusions. He's probably an upstanding journalist."

"Famous last words," whispered Marie.

I came to serve coffee and delicious pastries to the group and overheard the Geezers' discussions. I added to their conversation. "Look, everyone, don't be spreading rumors. I met Cameron, and he seemed to be a reputable man. Yes, Sadie and Lola are a bit enamored, but you know how dramatic Lola is, and Sadie needs a bit of hope in her life. Sheriff Hoffman certainly hasn't made any moves toward her in the romance department. Let it go. I'm a good judge of character."

As I gave Cameron the okay, I didn't mention my suspicions when I observed his distrusting look when he heard Mr. Brump was a former police officer. *I hope my recommendation isn't off base.*

Edna Mae said, "It looks like we got off track on our discussion of the book *Deception*, but maybe the theme of deception has permeated our discussion of the journalist's intentions. Let's hope he's not deceiving us."

When the book club members left, I remembered my promise to meet Lola for dinner. I also wanted to hear about Sadie's breakfast with Sheriff Houtman. Did Sadie tell him about Billy's nightmare, and if the sheriff was going to question Billy again? I was tired by the time I locked the store at 5:30. I hurried home, checked on Asher and Mike, and listened to several phone messages. One was from Matt who had just returned to Kentucky to get his boys ready to make a move here this weekend. I smiled as I heard Matt's voice. I was glad his boys agreed to the move. I hope they like the house I picked out for them. Matt agreed with my choice after he looked at the photos of each room online. He already made an offer to the realtor, and they are going to sign the contract on Saturday.

After checking my email, I headed to dinner. I was a little anxious about what Lola had in mind, but I love that girl like the daughter I never had, so I was excited to hear Lola's plans.

Chapter 24

Lola Is Excited About Her Future

That evening at Sweet Indulgences, after we ordered a delicious meal with hummus as an appetizer and a main dish of Koussa, stuffed zucchini, Lola got down to business and began to tell us about her project. We were interrupted by Deputy Murphy entering the restaurant. He spotted our group, smiled, and approached our table. "Well, ladies, I just stopped in for a piece of Sadie's delicious coconut cream pie. Mind if I join you?"

As he said that, Murphy grabbed a chair and proceeded to sit it at our table.

I saw this action as being rather bold, but Lola's face lit up with joy when he joined us. *Maybe she likes Murphy more than just a little.*

"How's your day going, Robert?" said Lola.

"Much better now," said Murphy. "Earlier, I had a bit of a dispute with the sheriff about scheduling. I'm fed up with him ignoring the fact that I have a life too. Would you believe, he doesn't even know my first name? Sometimes, he's so self-centered and opinionated."

Sadie jumped in and tried to defend the sheriff, but Lola and I agreed with Robert's assessment of the sheriff's personality. Sadie was silent after her defense of Mark.

Lola changed the direction of the conversation when she saw how defensive Sadie was. "Robert, you're just in time to hear my plans for starting a new career right here in Pittman. I've been thinking seriously about my future. I'm twenty-three, and it's time I have some direction in my life. I've decided to put my experience with acting and my love of children into opening an Acting Studio offering classes in Improv, Children's Theater, Set Design, Stage Managing, Musical Theater, Writing and Composing Scripts, and finally Dance Therapy to Relieve Stress."

Lola handed out a Business Plan that included detailed plans for each of the classes including the price, curriculum for each, and the intended audience. She also included her description of what she envisioned for the studio, how large it needed to be, the configuration of the rooms and stage or stages, and the capacity needed for the number of clients she expected to attract. Her goal in the long run is for the studio to become an integral part of the theater scene in the Berkshires, providing education and training for aspiring actors and script writers. It would also complement and feed into Matt Clare's plans for a new Children's Theater.

"What do you think?" Lola looked at us with an air of expectation seeking our approval and input.

After a pause to digest all this information, I said, "I think this is a great plan. You'll be using all your acting experience and filling an educational void here in Pittman that will be of value to the whole Berkshire Theater Scene."

"Do you have the money for this venture?" asked

Deputy Murphy. "A plus is that you will be staying in Pittman. I am glad of that." Robert's gaze could only be interpreted by all as infatuation with Lola.

Lola blushed at his comments. "I have some money that I inherited from my mother that I have been saving for this very venture."

"Is there a store available on Farley Square or nearby?" asked Robert.

"Before you jump in to purchase a store," Sadie said, "maybe you could tweak your business plans and go into more depth on the details. I'll be glad to help you with that."

I said, "We could still check with the Farley Square Merchants' Society and see if any of the stores are being put on the market soon. There's a meeting tomorrow night so I could ask them for you, or you could attend with me."

"I'd appreciate you asking for me, Robin. I'm trying not to spread myself too thin. I need all my energy to give a stellar performance as Kate at Shakespeare and Company.

"In my spare time (ha, ha), I have an interim plan for my business until a store goes up for rent, if you agree, Robin?" Lola said. "If we can remodel your office at the Bookworm Shop, I could offer small group classes, and I could purchase some new chairs and tables for the Story Corner that could be used for small group classes and an informal setting for a cabaret to offer participants a place for impromptu theater. I will pay the expenses for the remodeling and collect the money from these ventures to help with the expenses. Sadie, I can offer snacks catered by Sweet Indulgences for those watching performances on the stage. Robert, since you're out and about town, you could maybe help with publicity and spread the word about what is being offered. What do you all think?"

I said, "Again, it's a little early to jump right in with our opinions since this is the first we are hearing about all of this. My initial reaction is incredibly positive."

"I agree. It sounds like a great idea, but the details are going to need expanding," said Sadie.

"I also agree. It sounds like a great idea, but very ambitious. Just be careful you don't spread yourself too thin and have no time for other things such as acting at the Playhouse and dating. I will be glad to do whatever publicity you need, and take care of the dating situation," said Robert Murphy, trying to hide his blush.

"I told them all that Matt Clare was returning to Pittman with his boys tomorrow so they could enroll in the high school. Why don't you show Matt your business plan and see what he says since it could complement his plans for a Children's Theater? Being an experienced businessman, he might be willing to give you some input and help. Why don't you also print out these plans, so we can take some time to study them."

I continued, "As for using my store in the interim, attach any monetary outlay by you and by me that will be required. For instance, the price of the chairs, fees you will charge, hours you will be open, etc. The more details you can give, the stronger your plan will be. Also, include the hours you will be able to work in my bookstore since this new venture will mean I will have to rethink my staffing needs."

"Okay," Lola said. "Robin, I know this puts you in

a bind. I don't mean to leave you in the lurch. I see this initial venture as an extension of your offerings at the Bookworm Shop. Thanks everyone for your encouragement. It will take some time to get these details together, and I need some time management to pull all this off, but I'm excited that I finally see a purpose in my life."

The food arrived. "Robert, we have quite enough for all of us, so dig right in," said Sadie. We turned to our wonderful selection of entrees and enjoyed our dinner. "Nothing like knowing the restaurant owner," I said. As we ate, our talk turned to the upcoming Ski Fest.

Robert told us of the sheriff's concern about safety. "He doesn't realize how thin he is stretching his small staff. He needs to hire another deputy. Do you think Mr. Brump with his experience in law enforcement would be interested in becoming a consultant or part-time investigator?

We all considered this but felt that none of us could answer for Mr. Brump. I said, "I think, Robert, you'll have to ask him yourself."

After a fruitful discussion and a great meal, we had some positive plans for the future though everything will need further work. We all felt exhausted but refreshed and hopeful. Goodnights were said by all, and we headed home.

Chapter 25

The Meeting of the Farley Square Merchants' Society

When I went into the meeting, I added Lola's request to the New Business Agenda.

Sadie and I grabbed seats together. Sadie looked beautiful as always. I looked tired. "I wonder if I will ever again feel not tired?"

"Robin, you just do too much. If Lola's plan goes through, you are going to have to get some help in the bookstore. You spread yourself too thin by working full-time. Edna Mae loves running the cash register and helping all your customers. Why don't you ask for her part-time help? That way you will have more time to take part in activities with the band parents, and for raising your son Asher, and Mike. On top of all that, you also direct or participate in all the neighborhood activities. Maybe Matt coming to town will force you to relax and think about your own well-being. I'm sure Edna would enjoy having something to do that would use her talents."

"I just wish the sheriff could solve the shooting at Tanglewood. I hate the idea of the boys running around freely when there is a potential murderer in our midst."

The chairman called the meeting to order. When the merchants came to the new business on the agenda,

I asked if any storefronts might be available in the next few months. I then explained why Lola would like to purchase a storefront on Farley Square or one at least near the theater district.

The owner of the photo supply store spoke up. "I have been debating about whether I will need to sell my shop because of a downturn in sales. I am not ready to retire yet, but these new cameras are very self-sufficient and don't need as many supplies as before. I would be willing to talk to Lola about a type of partnership to see if we could work out a plan that would allow her studio and my camera supply business to coexist and complement each other. However, I have been approached by another possible buyer, Andy, Cameron Coldren's photographer. He is considering a permanent location to open his own photography business. Nothing is definite though."

Ms. Bowman said, "I might have to close my candy shop after my son goes off to college. It's difficult for me now to make the candy because my arthritis has flared up. I've been putting off telling my family because I love that store. It's been special to my family because every one of my children and siblings has worked in the shop, but I am fond of Lola and wouldn't feel bad if she were the new owner. Let me talk to my family, and I'll get back to you all."

The chairman of the committee said, "Let's let these people talk to Lola after they make some difficult decisions, and let's have them report at our next meeting. Also, if any others are considering selling, let the committee know or talk to Ms. George, and she will relay the information to Lola. It's a delight to see a talented young person like Lola wanting to stay in

Pittman and open a business. I think all of you can take some of the credit for making this town a welcoming community."

I said, "I thank everyone, but reiterate that all of Lola's plans are tentative and rely on certain decisions lining up just right." After the treasurer's report, the chairman adjourned the meeting.

I said to Sadie, "This should make Lola happy, and she doesn't have to make a hasty decision. She'll have time to think through the whole venture a little more, and it will give me extra time to plan for the transition."

"Agreed. Now, let's go home and get some much-needed sleep. You can talk to Lola tomorrow."

Chapter 26

Mr. Brump, the Grump

I know that they all call me a grump, but what my acquaintances don't know is that I deliberately adopted a persona as a grump. That way people leave me alone and even avoid me.

My mission is to observe and detect. That's what I did most of my career, and it's served me well. My wife used to laugh at me. "If you would just quit being so grouchy, you might get promoted. But no, you enjoy being a grump." She was right. Grouchiness is the perfect cover. People leave me alone, and suspects are afraid of me when I question them. They usually break down and then confess quickly.

Observe and detect. This has worked well here in Pittman. I thought this would be the perfect place to retire after my wife died. I took care of her for three long years through her bout with cancer. Now I want a peaceful spot to spend my retirement and maybe lose the grumpiness and make some friends. That's why I joined the Geezer Book Club. I love to read and have even toyed with the idea of writing a mystery novel set in Pittman.

I was just about ready to start changing my personality when I discovered some underlying sinister happenings in our small town.

First, I observed these three twelve-year-old boys who decided to harass the elders in our neighborhood. They would pull pranks, like moving the senior citizens' porch furniture to their front lawns, stealing statues from their gardens, and putting their statues on the town square. They also changed around the signs in the elders' vegetable gardens so they were surprised when strawberries grew instead of lettuce. I'm sure the boys thought these pranks were harmless and funny, but they made life difficult for the elderly.

I managed one day to get close enough to look into one of the boys' eyes. Sure enough, his pupils were dilated, a sure sign of drug use. I was determined to figure out where they were getting drugs. I could hear my wife's voice, "Dear, just leave it to the local police. Enjoy your retirement."

The second problem I was obsessed with was figuring out the elusive Lola. She isn't yet aware that I recognize her from Chicago. I was the detective who called her to Grant Park to identify her mom's body. Her mom died of a drug overdose. After Lola identified the body, she just said for us to bury her mom, or cremate her, or whatever. She didn't care, and she wasn't going to pay for the burial since she couldn't afford it. Then before I could have her talk to a social worker, she disappeared quickly. When we checked out her mom's apartment, we found nothing disturbed and no sign of forced entry. I expect that Lola went to the apartment and took whatever she wanted.

How did she end up in Pittman, and how does she have enough money to be thinking about opening an acting studio? She either is our thief and has been stealing from the money boxes, or she stole the instruments and sold them, or there was a stash of jewels or money at her mom's apartment. If any of those scenarios are true, I intend to find out by observing and detecting them.

My third problem has to do with two recent arrivals in Pittman who seem to be suspicious. No one seems to know much about their past lives. Cameron Coldren is a journalist and has produced podcasts and several Video Documentary Series for the past four years, but I can't find any record of his activities before that time. Horatio Nelson also arrived in town a year ago and opened Nelson's Pet Shop, but I can't find any record of any previous businesses, or where he lived before. I need to keep up my grumpy persona until I uncover the solutions to these mysteries.

Chapter 27

We're Ready

At the next meeting of the Ski Fest Planning Committee, each group reported the progress they had made. Though the Fest wasn't until November, it takes a long time to coordinate volunteers and their responsibilities. Thankfully, all the volunteers were ready to put in the work needed to make the fest successful.

Food Booths:

Sadie and Edna Mae said they now had five food booths.

—Ice Cream Delights—Sweet Indulgences was providing ice cream, and Lola would run that booth.

—Tour the Middle East—This booth will be run by Sadie, Mr. Habbib, and Ali, who has bragged about his cooking prowess. Sadie hadn't yet tested his cooking, but he certainly likes to eat. The booth will feature pita sandwiches with lamb, chicken, or beef, and phitia, which is a meat pie, and kibbeh and salad.

—Marie's Southern Barbeque–This will serve barbeque sandwiches and coleslaw, hamburgers, metts, and grilled vegetables. Mike and Bart O'Neal, who is a master at grilling, will man the booth.

—The Cake Palace–Marie will feature her sumptuous cakes and cupcakes. Edna Mae will assist her. "We might even convince Edna to put an apron over her fancy clothes," said Sadie.

—The Snack Shack–Run by Milo and Ms. Caster, the manager at Jiminy Creak, this booth will also double as the main ticket booth. Hopefully, guests will not only pay their entrance fee but also pick up some cotton candy and freshly popped caramel corn to eat as they browse the other displays and activities at the Fest.

"Mmmmm," said Billy, and the whole group echoed his sentiment as they licked their lips.

Billy and Wayne reported on which booths will be displaying and selling their wares, and which activities will take place.

Asher and Mike explained the financial details. "Revenues will come from booth rentals, entrance fees, and a percentage of sales," said Mike. "Each booth will donate a percentage of their profits from the day's sales which will go to the Ski venues of Jiminy Peak and Bousquet Ski Area to help defray expenses this season. The fees of fifty dollars a booth, five dollars entry fees, and money from a raffle will go to the ski venues to subsidize daily entrance fees for locals who need financial assistance and subsidize fees for any kids who need assistance to pay for team activities such as racing teams for middle graders and high schoolers. These fees will also help pay for ski lessons and equipment for all young people whose parents are having trouble meeting these expenses.

Asher continued the report. "Wayne and Billy have chosen to raffle off an adult racing bike and a child's beginning two-wheeler with training wheels. Ms. Caster from Jiminy Peak has agreed to raffle a set of skis and ski boots. Bousquet Ski Club will raffle off two things:

One will be a Pickle Ball racket, and they will sign up anyone interested in taking lessons or joining a Pickleball Team offered at the Berkshire gym across from the Ski Lodge. Another raffle will be for a child's seasonal pass to ski at Bousquet.

"Wow, these raffles should bring in a lot of money," said Lola. Everyone agreed.

As plans came together, I was proud of my town. It reminded me of my Kentucky home where neighbors came together as a family community.

****

After spending a restless night after the closing of the Adventure Park, I snarled out loud to the empty room, "I hate that man. I could kill Horatio Nelson. Abusing a teenager like that." I could barely choke down my breakfast because I was so upset. Finding a tennis ball of Asher's, I marched down the street and hurled it into the alley behind Sweet Indulgences. "If it works for Sadie, maybe it will work for me too," I mumbled.

One, two....ten....twenty....one hundred." I shouted the numbers as I hit the trash can. *I'm still not calm. What works for the Lebanese, must not work for Kentuckians*. I closed my eyes, and when I looked up, I saw Sheriff Houtman rushing into the alley.

"Robin, are you okay? I thought it was Sadie venting again. I didn't know hitting a trash can with a ball was therapy for all women."

"Well, what do you expect? Once again, I hear that you are about to accuse the wrong person, a young man who can't defend himself. Why do you think you should arrest Milo for the thefts and/or the shooting at Tanglewood? What about Cameron Coldren or Wayne?

We know nothing about Cameron, and he was seen among the booths as the park was closing and so was Wayne. I guess I'm going to have to fire up the investigative powers of the Super Sleuths again."

"I was just wanting to make sure you and Sadie are okay," said a surprised sheriff.

"Oh, let it go, sheriff. There are other ways to woo Sadie. She doesn't need a rescuer and neither do I." I stomped off leaving a bewildered lawman in my wake.

****

The sheriff and Deputy Murphy were steeped in paperwork when Sadie and I went to ask their help in investigating Wayne. As we started to fill the two lawmen in, Miss Caster, the manager at Jiminy Peak, burst through the door of the station, ignoring Sadie and me. She went right up to Deputy Murphy and Sheriff Houtman. The sheriff could see that Ms. Caster was very upset so he said, "Ms. Caster, why don't we speak privately in another room."

When they moved to another room, Ms. Caster demanded he arrest Milo Nelson. Though he was surprised at her aggressive behavior, he listened to her demands. "Ms. Caster, your argument is convincing. Deputy Murphy and I have already questioned Milo, but we will definitely investigate this situation further. Now leave it to us and return to Jiminy Peak. We'll let you know what we find out."

When Ms. Caster left the station, the sheriff asked Sadie and me to return to the station later.

I said to Sadie," What do you think is going on? It's not like him to cut us short. I wonder what Ms. Caster is upset about." We left and went back to Sadie's restaurant for breakfast, agreeing to try again with the sheriff later.

Finding Ms. Caster's accusation that Milo had been the thief at the closing party at the Adventure Park believable, coupled with his being seen at the high school band room, Sheriff Houtman and Deputy Murphy went to again question Milo Nelson. They found him alone at his house. His father was probably at the pet store. He didn't answer his phone when they tried to warn Horatio Nelson that they intended to question his son.

The sheriff told Deputy Murphy to take Milo to the station, anyway. When they all returned, Sheriff Houtman sat Milo down and began questioning him. The sheriff hoped to get him to confess to the thefts. At first, Milo refused to say anything and just glared at the sheriff. The sheriff began asking specific questions about each robbery and presenting reasons why he was accusing him. Milo didn't protest. He just hung his head and looked thoroughly depressed. As the sheriff went on with his questions, Milo just kept shaking his head, but eventually caved in and broke down in tears. "Stop, stop. I did it." He admitted to all the thefts.

"But why would you steal from your neighbors and friends?"

"I'm sorry, sheriff. I needed money," said Milo.

"Why did you need money, Milo? You are constantly working. You seldom spend any money. What did you need the money for?"

Milo sobbed. "I-I just needed to run away. I can't take my dad's beatings and verbal abuse anymore. I even thought about shooting him. When he threatened me with that ugly snake, I was terrified. I sold the instruments and other things I managed to steal from other businesses. I have the money I stole from these thefts and the cash boxes at the adventure park in my backpack that is at my house hidden in my closet. They are my getaway funds."

Sheriff Houtman was stunned. He wasn't sure what to make of this confession or what to do with this poor child. He couldn't send him home to his dad, and if he asked Nelson about it, it would only make it worse for Milo. "I have to ask you about the shooting at Tanglewood. We noticed you arrived late for the concert. You would have been in a good position to line up a shot with a rifle. Did you have anything to do with the attempted assassination?"

"No, sheriff. I swear. I would never shoot anyone. I just fantasize about shooting my dad, but I would never do it. I couldn't kill anyone. Please believe me. I've confessed to the thefts and told you why. I'm so sorry. But I didn't try to shoot my dad or anyone else. Please believe me."

Mark and his deputy debated their choices. They put the still sobbing teenager in a holding cell and came to see Sadie and me. Though he was loathe to ask for help, Mark knew he needed the perspective of a mother or someone who understands teenagers. Sheriff Houtman hoped he would be able to come up with an answer to his dilemma. He sure hated to show weakness in front of Sadie and admit that she was right, and he was wrong, but a boy's welfare was at stake.

Sheriff Houtman entered Sweet Indulgences just as I was about to leave. He was in a huff and refused to look directly at Sadie. "You ladies will be pleased to know that Deputy Murphy and I have solved the mystery of the thefts. We are holding Milo Nelson until we can talk to his father.

Ms. Caster spotted Milo slinking around the booths at Jiminy Peak. Ms. White, the band director, also saw him near the band room when the band instruments disappeared. Mr. Brump, hired by Ms. Caster for security the last weekend at the Adventure Park, confirmed that Milo was wandering around the booths at the Adventure Park. Milo offered no alibi.

"Why would Milo need money?" asked Sadie. "He works at the pet shop every day after school and on weekends. As far as I know, he doesn't spend a lot of money. This is ridiculous. sheriff, you must be wrong."

"Sadie, after further questioning, Milo finally broke down and confessed to the thefts. I'm sure you don't trust my judgement. Maybe you should ask your journalist friend what he thinks since he seems so smart and trustworthy. So much for coming to ask you two for help." With that speech, Sheriff Houtman stormed out the door. He joined Deputy Murphy at the station, and they marched to Milo's house to confront Horatio Nelson.

Sadie looked at me when Mark left. "Maybe we need to gather our sleuths together to prove Milo's innocence."

"Let's give the sheriff a chance," I said. "He already thinks we are busybodies, and now he's jealous of Cameron. Maybe we should wait and see what happens."

****

Mr. Nelson had already gotten wind of the fact that the sheriff had taken his son in for questioning. He feared that the sheriff also was planning to search their house. Nelson met the sheriff and his deputy at the door sporting a rifle on his hip. "Just what do you all think you're doing? You kidnap my son and take him to jail then arrive here intending to search our home. Do you think we live in a dictatorship? I have rights. No one is allowed to question a minor without a parent or another adult present, and it is illegal to search my premises without a warrant. Do you have a warrant?"

The sheriff was enraged. "Who does this man think he is?" he said to Murphy. Then he turned and stomped down the street back to his car to go for a warrant, leaving Murphy there to make sure Nelson didn't try to get rid of any evidence.

When he returned with the warrant, both lawmen searched everywhere and found nothing. They needed evidence to add to the confession of a minor if they were to arrest Milo and make a strong enough argument for the arrest to hold.

Once back at the jail, Houtman released Milo with a warning, "Young man, we will be watching you very carefully. We will consider your confession and collect the needed evidence, then we will revisit these charges. You are released pending a hearing and are to go immediately home. Your father wants to see you. Don't do anything violent or even suspicious, or you will be right back in a jail cell. If your father tries to punish you in any way, or gets abusive, you call me. Here's my number."

Milo left shaking and fearful, then headed to the park to sit before he had to face his awful father.

Chapter 28

Murder

The City Council had almost canceled Halloween for Trick or Treaters because of the poor air quality. The still-burning fires in Quebec were causing air quality alerts never before seen in the Berkshires. The parents, however, protested so the council allowed the kids to go out with adult supervision but only for two hours. The parents agreed to these restrictions.

Mr. Habbib was taking Ahmram out for his first Halloween in the USA, so he agreed to take a group of kids from his neighborhood along so the parents could stay home and hand out treats. Ali agreed to stay at the house and give out candy and pennies to any visitors.

****

This dark Halloween night was perfect for the assassin to carry out his assignment. If anyone saw him skulking around, they wouldn't even notice him. The disguised assassin approached the pet shop just as Mr. Nelson was about to put up the Closed sign.

"Well, I'm surprised you are shopping on such a foggy night. Good costume, by the way. I was just about to close early. What kind of animal are you interested in? We have everything from domestic cats and dogs to exotic parrots and snakes."

"I would like to see your boa constrictors," said the mysterious customer.

"These cages over here hold our extensive snake collection. Would you like to hold one of the boas?"

"Sure," the assassin said.

When Horatio Nelson went behind the counter to open the boa's cage, the assassin checked the store for observers. When he was satisfied, they were alone, the man swung the hammer hard onto the back of Nelson's head. Nelson fell and cracked his face on the glass display case.

Blood splashed everywhere. The hitman, careful to avoid the blood, checked for a pulse. When he determined the abusive storekeeper was dead, the assassin grabbed one of the boas and then dragged Horatio's body to the back storeroom. No one could see the blood through the windows because it was behind the display cases, so the assassin just left it undisturbed.

Wrapping the boa around Nelson's neck, he wiped any fingerprints off the hammer. The assassin threw the hammer into a backpack that was sitting on the storeroom floor. Then the murderer snapped a picture of the scene, turned off the store lights, and quietly slipped out the back door into the alley walking away into the darkness. He was satisfied that his assignment was complete, and the photo would be his proof.

Now, on to the next assignment, which is proving to be much more difficult. It's a good thing there is no immediate timeline for these two next assassinations. Now that I have completed the drug dealer's assignment, I can give him the proof of the deed being accomplished and collect the rest of my payoff. I should then be able to buy some time to get ready for the next assassination commissioned by the ISIS leader, Aresh.

Meanwhile, Milo Nelson, after being released by the sheriff, went home and was about to heat a frozen dinner when he realized he had left his backpack behind in the storeroom earlier today.

I can't let my dad find my backpack. I'm sunk if he goes through the contents and finds my getaway money.

Milo went back to the pet shop. When he got to the darkened store, Milo took out his keys to unlock the front door but was surprised to find the door was unlocked.

I don't get it. If I left the door unlocked, my dad would kill me, but he was supposed to close tonight, and Mr. 'Never Makes a Mistake' Nelson left the door unlocked. Ha. Mr. Horatio Nelson isn't such a perfect person after all.

Milo switched on the lights as he entered the dark store. He stepped behind the cases headed to the storeroom and slipped. Milo fell hard on his knees, and blood covered his hands and the knees of his jeans.

"What the…!" Milo screamed to the empty store. As he got up, he spotted all the blood on the tiled floor. He cringed when he saw his dad's body, face down, spread eagle

Petrified, Milo ran to him. "Dad, wake up. Dad!" he cried as he shook his dad's bloody shoulders.

That's when he spotted the boa looped around Nelson's neck like a gray scarf. Milo backed away, shaking. He screamed again.

Mr. Habbib was passing the pet store as he was supervising the trick-or-treaters. When he heard the bloodcurdling screams, he called Sadie's house for help. He needed her to come and supervise the kids so he could leave them and go into the store to investigate. Sadie wasn't home, but Aunt Florence answered and said, "I will call 911, then I'll be right there. I'm only a few blocks away."

Mr. Habbib instructed the kids to stay right there on the sidewalk until Aunt Florence arrived. He slowly opened the front door of the shop and headed toward the screaming.

He spotted the boy screaming. "Milo, Milo, calm down. What has happened?" Milo ran into Mr. Habbib's arms, shaking and sobbing. Mr. Habbib held him and stroked his head. "There, there," he said to the stricken boy. "It's okay. I've got you. Whatever has happened, you are safe."

That's when Mr. Habbib noticed the blood on Milo. The hysterical child clung to him, so Omar waited for law enforcement to arrive and investigate.

When Sheriff Houtman and Deputy Murphy arrived at the pet store, they saw a nervous Mr. Habbib holding Milo, and both were covered in blood. "What's happened here?" asked the sheriff, "and where did all this blood come from?"

Mr. Omar Habbib, still holding the sobbing child, pointed to the floor behind the display cases.

The two lawmen approached cautiously. That's when they discovered the corpse. Deputy Murphy asked, "Who is it?"

"It appears someone has attacked Horatio Nelson. There's a massive amount of blood oozing from the wound on the back of his head. Murphy, you take Milo from Mr. Habbib and get him cleaned up and, hopefully, calmed down. Meanwhile, I'll question Omar Habbib."

The sheriff said, "Milo, let go. It's going to be all right. Deputy Murphy will take your hand and make sure you are safe. I just want you to tell us what you saw. Now, calm down and quietly go with Deputy

Murphy."

Sheriff Hoffman made a quick call and then said to his deputy, "I just called in a forensic team from Albany to examine the murder scene. As soon as they get started, I'll meet you and Milo at the station."

The sheriff turned to the boy. "Milo, did you ever have any supper tonight?" Milo shrugged and shook his head. "Deputy Murphy, do you think on the way to the station you can pick something up for the boy? I'm sure that will calm him down."

Deputy Murphy said, "Milo, do you like hamburgers?" Still shaking, Milo nodded and walked closer to Deputy Murphy as they headed to the police car.

After hearing Mr. Habbib's account of what happened, the sheriff told him he could leave, but to stay in town until this is resolved. When Omar left the pet shop, he headed to Aunt Florence's house to pick up the confused children. What had started out as a joyous Halloween night had turned into a nightmare. He was sure that Ahmram would be terrified if he remembered any of his ordeals in Lebanon with the invaders.

****

As the sheriff waited for the forensic team to arrive, he phoned Robin to ask her to sit in as a surrogate parent for legal reasons. He knew he couldn't question anyone under eighteen without an adult present. "Robin, we have a situation. Milo found a dead body in the pet shop, and I need to question him. Could you or Sadie sit in as an adult observer?"

"Why can't Milo's father be present?"

"Horatio Nelson is dead. It appears he may have been murdered."

"What? Don't tell me you suspect his son? There is no way Milo would do anything like that," I said.

"Calm down. Milo was in the store and was covered in blood. I need to get specifics on what happened. At this point, I need to find out how this went down. Why do you always jump to conclusions about my competency? It's about time you and your friends started trusting me. Now, are you going to help or just be a pain in my butt?"

The sheriff sounded angry, but he also sounded like he desperately needed help so I gave in. "Okay, sheriff, I'll be right down."

After the forensic team took over, Sheriff Houtman headed back to the station to question Milo. *Hopefully, Robin will be there by now.*

****

Deputy Murphy was just leading Milo into the station when he spotted me arriving to look after him.

I rushed up to the stricken boy. "Milo, it's okay. I'm going to be right by your side. I see you got some food. Let's go over to that table and give you a chance to eat while I talk to the sheriff. He just got here, so I will go into his office to talk to him. Then he will want to ask you some questions."

I left Milo and entered the office. "Sheriff Hoffman, you know that Milo would never kill his father. Though Nelson did abuse Milo, he was still his father. Milo had a love/hate relationship with him. Being an only child with no mother around, he had only his father to rely on."

"But, Robin, you're forgetting that Milo has admitted that he stole all that money because he was planning to run away. He could have chosen to eliminate his dad, then he wouldn't have to run away."

"No, I don't believe that. Check with Mr. Habbib who witnessed the whole scene."

"He's coming down to the station for questioning as soon as he gets the trick-or-treaters he was escorting back to their parents and finds a babysitter for Ahmram. Hopefully, Ali is home and can watch Ahmram."

The sheriff continued, "Robin, I intend to solve this murder quickly. Please don't interfere."

When the sheriff questioned him, Mr. Habbib insisted that Milo couldn't be the killer. "The sobbing boy I held could never have killed his father."

The sheriff believed Mr. Habbib's eyewitness statement and Milo's determined denial. He released Milo into Omar Habbib's custody.

Chapter 29

Will He Cancel?

Cameron Coldren came into the bookstore with Andy when Lola was just ending her shift. She invited them both to sit in the reading room so they could discuss his concerns.

"Lola, I fear for the future of our collaboration on this podcast and video broadcast. At the very least, I need to change direction. Our theme of a quaint and serene small town in contrast to the big cities is dashed by all this current crime. If I continue, I will redirect my focus to the theme that violence and mayhem can exist in small towns as well as in the big city."

"But if you do that, Cameron, it will reduce tourism that we count on. The reputation of the Berkshires as a destination for all theater lovers as well as skiers will be ruined. You need to reconsider. Give us time to talk to our committee on community affairs and to our stubborn sheriff. Please don't broadcast any rumors that will ruin our businesses. I suggest if you need to change your focus, you change your angle to the resilience of people when faced with danger, no matter where they live."

Andy said, "I like that idea, Cameron. I have lots of footage featuring the many people who have moved to Pittman and the locals who grew up here. This new focus might work. We could interview people about how they face their fears of danger and why they find Pittman a better place to confront fear than the big cities."

Lola said, "You also need to know that Robin and I are going to consult our lawyer if you do print or broadcast anything about the crimes. We all agreed to the video broadcast about the beauty of living in a small town. Any change of direction could be considered a breach of contract. Mind you, we don't want to sue for any reason, but we will if we must. Let's please put any concerns on hold. Give us five days, and we'll talk again with our committee, our lawyer, and our sheriff present."

Cameron was a bit taken aback by Lola's firmness and familiarity with the law. *She is not going to be a pushover. Little does she know about my other reasons for pulling out of this project. I better play along before she finds out my ulterior motive for this whole project.*

"Okay, Lola, you win. We will all meet five days from now. Check with Robin, and you set the time and place. That will give you time to contact the others." With those words, Cameron stomped out of the shop, and Andy meekly followed.

Chapter 30

Wayne

Searching for another suspect for the Tanglewood shooting and Nelson's murder, I went to Sadie's house that night to ask Billy and Sadie some questions about Wayne, who also was seen walking around at Tanglewood. "What do you know about Wayne's background? Billy, you went into a partnership with Wayne. Why?"

"Well," said Billy, "Asher and Mike were in a band with Wayne for two years, and they said he was a decent guy who always had a passion for motorcycles. I think his dad owned an auto repair shop somewhere in the Berkshires."

"Sadie, did you or Billy check Wayne's credit and bank accounts?"

"Uh, no," said Sadie. "Billy was determined to enter into the partnership so I just trusted him to check everything out with Mr. Wright, the lawyer at Wright and Peterson's who was handling Billy's inheritance, and with the manager at the bank who worked with Mr. Wright to deposit the money in Billy's account.

Billy said, "I did ask Mr. Wright's advice. He seemed to think it was a sound investment."

"Did you check Wayne's credit ratings, etc.?"

"No," Billy said, "I asked Mr. Wright about that,

but he said the bank manager told him since Wayne was investing cash, a background check wasn't necessary."

Sadie was puzzled. "I didn't know Wayne was investing cash. Where would a kid who just graduated last year get that kind of cash?"

"Billy," I asked, "do you think Wayne would be capable of murder? Do you think he had any problems with Nelson?"

"I honestly don't know what to think about Wayne right now. With his evasiveness and his disappearances, I just can't vouch for him anymore."

The three of us decided to pose these exact questions to the sheriff.

****

Billy met with Asher and Mike and told them that he was worried about Wayne's frequent absences and that they might have something to do with illegal activities. "Last night, I had a horrid nightmare about Wayne throwing money from the bike shop's cash register all around the room. In my nightmare, the sheriff showed up, caught the cash, and arrested Wayne and me for theft. My shop was all boarded up as we were hauled off to jail. When I woke up, I was sweating and staring at my pajamas, wondering why they didn't have prison stripes on them."

"What an imagination," said Asher.

"But it was so real. I was covered in sweat," Billy said.

Mike and Asher both encouraged Billy to confront Wayne. "Obviously," they said, "you are more worried than you realized about Wayne's suspicious activities." I agreed to confront him soon. "Thanks for the advice."

Monday night, before Billy went to his shift at the

store, he decided to confront Wayne. "Wayne, we need to talk. I just reviewed the sales figures for August and September, and there is a big problem. You need to explain to me why there is such a discrepancy in sales from what I expected to see and the actual sales recorded."

Wayne was less than transparent. He tried to just brush aside any of Billy's concerns. "Don't get all excited, Billy, I'm just trying to better our business. I go on speaking engagements at many sales conventions to try to drum up business for our mail-order sales. This is a great advertising tool. The money I bring back is from speaking fees at the various conventions."

"Why would they pay you a fee if you are advertising our website? Also, that's a lot of conventions. How do you find these destinations?"

"I've joined a speaker's bureau, and they book the venues and pay me to give talks on everything from the benefits of exercise to the wonders of traveling. My next speech is, 'See the Marvels of the USA by Traveling on a Motorcycle.' These talks are well funded, and now that I am getting known on the speaking circuit, I am in demand. All of this is good for our business."

"Why is this the first I'm hearing about this?" asked a puzzled Billy.

"I wanted to be sure it would prove lucrative before I told you. I've never been a speaker before, and I wanted to see if I could make a success of this venture before I told you. I always put my speaking fees back in the business receipts to make up for the time gone."

"If you plan to continue this venture, Wayne, three things need to happen. One, you need to put all the times you will be absent from the shop on the calendar ahead of time, so I am aware of what days you will be gone. If anything happens during the time you are gone, I have to be the designated person to call to handle the problem. Two, we need to hire someone to keep the shop open when you are gone, and I'm busy with school or band. We can't randomly be closing. We both must interview some candidates to take over the shop part-time when you are gone. We need to interview immediately so they will be ready to step in the next time you leave. Three, we need to itemize your speaking fees as income on our financial forms, or we will get into trouble with the IRS."

****

The next day, Billy related this whole conversation to Sadie and me. "Wayne agreed to all three terms, but I didn't like his reaction to all of this. I'm just not convinced, and I feel uncomfortable, like I don't believe his whole story or trust him. I asked him to make a video of his next speech so I'm aware of how our product is being presented. He didn't give me a clear answer."

I said, "It could be plausible, Billy. There are legitimate speakers' bureaus, and there are a lot of travel conventions and motorcycle groups, but why has he kept you in the dark? A video is an excellent idea."

"I agree, but why didn't he explain his plan to you to begin with, and why didn't he readily agree to the video? You are his equal partner and should be treated as such. That's the part I find suspicious," said Sadie.

"Have you checked your website sales recently? Has there been an uptick in sales since he started being absent?" I asked.

"At first, I didn't even know we had a website. When I left Wayne, I went back to the repair shop to check the website. It was created last year without my knowledge. There wasn't any record of any sales much less any increase in sales. I don't know. Maybe I'm being paranoid, and all of this is genuine. Wayne isn't very good at finance. He could just not know how to record sales." Billy turned to us and flailed his arms in a helpless gesture. "Any ideas about what to do next?"

"I think you or I should talk to Sheriff Houtman," Sadie said, "and have Wayne give you a list of everywhere he has spoken, and the sheriff can check if these speaking engagements are legitimate and actually took place, or if his whole story is a lie. Also, confront Wayne about the lack of sales figures on the website. See what he has to say."

"Okay, I hate to be so suspicious. It is plausible Wayne is telling the truth, but I'll feel better if the sheriff is willing to check this out for me. Thanks, Robin and Sadie, I can always count on you having my back."

Sadie hugged Billy, and we all went to eat dinner.

"Tomorrow will come soon enough, and while you're at school, I will try to go with Sadie to elicit the sheriff's help," I said.

Chapter 31

Tension Grips the Town

That night, I woke and sat up ramrod straight. I peered into my darkened room, lit only by a beam of moonlight.

What had awakened me? I listened, rubbed my tired eyes, and heard nothing. I crept to the window, freezing my toes on the cold floor. I lifted the slot of the wooden blind. Dark, quiet, nothing stirring. Then I laughed.

Robin, girl, I scolded myself, *this isn't a Christmas poem. You're not going to spot Santa on the lawn in his sleigh.* Then I heard it, a small cry, then another. Where was it coming from?

The night was calm, not a breeze was stirring. There, over by the fir tree, on a bench, a figure sat with her head in her arms, sobbing. Was it Sadie or Lola? Not Sadie. If she were upset, instead of crying, she'd be banging trash cans. It looks like Lola. Why is she in my yard, and why at (I glanced at my clock.) at three in the morning would she be out in the cold night? Should I go to her? I shook my head trying to clear my jumbled thoughts.

Lola chose that moment to rise, shake her shoulders, and start to leave. *Should I call out the window? No, I'd wake the neighbors, or at least Asher or Mike.* I decided to ask Lola in the morning. She could just be nervous because of her performances this weekend at Shakespeare and Company, or she could be spooked by the crimes in our usually peaceful town. I'll give her time to calm down. Her emotions could also be on edge due to sorting out her feelings about Deputy Murphy and Andy. *Ah, to be young and in love.*

I went back to my bed, climbed under my wildly colored quilt, and tried to get some sleep. I hated to be a grouch in the morning due to my lack of sleep. *I'll be glad when we can all throw aside our fears and feel peaceful again.*

****

When I finally drifted off to sleep, many images invaded my dreams.

First hitman hired–*If I don't go through with these two assignments, Aresh or the man in the trench coat will send someone to kill me. There's no backing out of this no matter how much I want to. Aresh made it clear that my marks were not negotiable. He told me that this was my first mission, and that I was to carry it out or else. I need to decide to walk away to my own death or my marks' deaths. Which will I choose?*

The drug lord–*This job needs to be finished right away. The hitman already botched his first attempt at Tanglewood. I am so angry that he attempted the assassination while I was attending the performance. He's gone back on his promise of a speedy hit. I canceled his contract, and I hired another more reliable assassin. No matter what, my identity must be protected, or else. How foolish was that botched attempt at Tanglewood, and how dangerous this whole thing has become. I need a better plan to protect myself, and I need a plan of escape if all else fails.*

Sadie–*I know that bullet at Tanglewood might have very well been meant for me. I knew ISIS would track me down one day. In the last year two people, Ali and Omar Habbib from my village in Lebanon, have tracked down my location. Omar said it was by chance that he found me when he came to eat at my Aunt Florence's restaurant, but I have no proof of that, only his word. If those two can find me, others can too.* Sadie went into protective mode. She cleaned her gun thoroughly and checked the batteries in her security cameras at home and at Sweet Indulgences. *She had to decide without scaring him how to warn Billy to be vigilant in case someone attempts to harm him.*

Asher—*I know the sheriff still thinks I could be guilty of the attempted assassination at Tanglewood even though he released me after my mother's demands and the lawyer's insistence. Does anyone else in town think I am guilty? I'm afraid to look people in the eye because I fear that they suspect me. I need to get on with my life. I haven't even submitted my application to college. Any more delays or suspicions and I can forget my future plans.*

Second hitman hired–*I need to get this done. You don't mess with a drug lord and live to talk about it, plus you don't mess with ISIS terrorists. They know who you are and where you live.*

Chapter 32

The Super Sleuths Convene Again

The next morning, I told Sadie about my dream. I told her that I also believe Mr. H.'s version of Nelson's death and can't believe that Milo is involved in any way in his dad's death. At the meeting of the Super Sleuths, we filled them in on the murder and the fact that the sheriff arrested Milo again and eventually released him.

"We need to find out who murdered Mr. Nelson so we can prove Milo innocent," I informed them. Mike, Billy, and Asher were quite shocked that the sheriff would accuse Milo. Yes, they knew that Milo had previously tried to leave town after he stole the money and sold the band instruments, but he confessed all of this to the sheriff. Where would he go if he skipped town?"

Billy said, "Sadie, remember the other day when I was in Sweet Indulgences, and Milo and I were having an intense discussion? I convinced Milo that he needed to avoid his dad as much as possible, but he must stay in town, or his dad would hunt him down, and there would be dire consequences. He agreed with me so I can't believe he would kill his dad. He knows he will never be free but will end up in prison. Milo isn't stupid; he's just a scared kid."

"Yeah, a scared but desperate kid who doesn't like

to have snakes thrown at him," growled Mike.

"Come on, Mike, we are supposed to be proving Milo innocent, not suspecting him. You are as bad as the sheriff," said Lola.

I was worried. Normally, when the Super Sleuths convene, they all agree with me, but I sensed a feeling that Mr. Nelson deserved to be murdered, and Milo might have done the killing as revenge, but worse was that several of the sleuths thought that he was justified in his decision.

Lola, returning from her meeting with Cameron and Andy, joined us.

For now, I said, "Let's focus on other suspects. Who else had a motive for the murder?"

Lola said, "Mr. Habbib has a motive. He doesn't like Nelson because he discovered that Nelson was planning to take over several businesses on Farley Square, and Omar Habbib was hoping to open a small grocery whenever a store went vacant. Nelson could have sabotaged Mr. Habbib's hope for a way to make a living doing something he loves."

I chimed in. "Nelson also was the one who accused Sadie of being an illegal alien and told her to go home to Lebanon. Several merchants noted his hatred of foreigners. Maybe Mr. Habbib. was defending Sadie. He seems to take an overwhelming interest in all things having to do with Sadie."

"Oh, Robin, that's not true. Omar Habbib just sees me as a friend," said Sadie.

Lola got up, pranced around the room, and sang, "Sadie's got a boyfriend. Sadie's got a beau. Sheriff Houtman isn't going to be happy." Then she bowed, and we all laughed. It felt good to lighten up a little.

Leave it to Lola.

Asher, ever the serious one, spoke up. "We need to get down to business. Milo is my friend, and I don't want him to spend another day in jail."

"Sorry, Asher. We all feel the same way, but I get anxious with all this serious talking about murder, and needed to lighten up a bit," said Lola.

"Let's all take a quick break and have some cookies, then we can get back to it," said Sadie.

When the sleuths got back to the table, they decided that Cameron was their next suspect. "What do we know about him?" asked Billy. "Does anyone know if he would have a motive?"

"That's the problem," said Mike. "All we know about him is that he is a podcaster and videographer, and he says he has been a journalist, but where and when?"

Lola was excited to report on the meeting she had with Cameron Coldren and Andy. "I just had a conversation with Cameron and Andy that I need to report to you all."

Cameron began, "Due to the thefts, the attempted assassination, and now a murder, we will need to change our focus of the videocast to 'people in small towns experience crimes and have fears just like the big cities.'

"I protested that if he changed that focus, he would be violating the contract we had with him for a videocast showing the advantage of small-town living. I also pointed out that he could ruin our tourist business. I told him we would consult a lawyer to find out how to sue him for damages from his reporting. I couldn't tell whether Cameron was relieved, angry, or confused by my reaction to his determination to change the focus of his reporting on our town. He agreed to wait five days so I could fill you all in and talk to our lawyer."

I asked, "Since he is thinking of changing the focus, could he have engineered the killing to give a sensational boost to his videocast and make a name for himself? The funny thing is I like him and his photographer. I don't think either one of them could commit murder."

Asher said, "At this point, liking him isn't the question. The question is did either of them have a motive for the killing. What is their connection to Mr. Nelson," said Asher. "We need to know if he has a connection to Nelson, or your theory doesn't work."

Sadie said, "Remember that the sheriff said he witnessed a raging argument between Cameron and Horatio Nelson. Could they be adversaries in a project or scheme, or know each other from a prior time before they both came to Pittman?"

Billy said, "Another potential suspect could be Ali. He's new to town, and why was he living in the Pittman Forest? Maybe he needed to be able to quickly disappear. Maybe someone paid him to murder Horatio. Ali certainly needed money."

While the group considered these possibilities, Sheriff Houtman entered Sweet Indulgences. He came to speak to Sadie, but when he saw the sleuths gathered around a table, he concluded that they were discussing his inability to solve a murder.

"Ladies and gentlemen, I have returned from interviewing several suspects. I have checked Omar Habbib's alibi, and I think we can clear him. Though he had experienced Nelson's hatred of immigrants firsthand, he also has a solid alibi for the time of the murder. The kids he was taking out for Halloween all told me the same story that Mr. H told them to stand on the corner until Sadie came to take them home. We also tested the blood on his clothes. The blood stains were consistent with the blood stains on Milo's shirt and hands and knees. It looks like Omar Habbib innocently hugged Milo to comfort the frantic boy, and that's how the blood was transferred to Mr. H's shirt. If Milo is indeed innocent, then we have to assume that Mr. H was just comforting a frightened child."

"If Milo is innocent? *IF*?" I shouted. "Why do you continue to refuse to recognize the obvious? There's no confusion here. Milo and Mr. Habbib are both innocent. You should be spending your time trying to find the real killer."

Sadie tried to calm me down, and I shrugged my shoulders and responded by sitting down in a huff.

"This is more complicated than some amateur sleuths are used to solving. You must leave the investigation to me," said the sheriff. "I need to get this murder solved and quickly. For a quiet town, my job just got more complicated than I bargained for. I can't let panic ensue because you've convinced people not to trust me to keep them safe. If you have any information about the murder, I should be the first person you notify. *No one else!*"

After that speech, the sheriff turned abruptly and left the restaurant, forgetting that he had called in an order for pick up.

"I just want this over with so that Cameron doesn't ruin our town with his new focus, and meanwhile, a killer is on the loose," I said to all the sleuths.

We adjourned to consider all the possibilities. We agreed to give the sheriff some more time.

Chapter 33

What About Feathers?

A few days later, Sheriff Houtman came into the Bookworm shop. Lola was at the checkout desk, so he decided to approach her with a request.

"Lola, could you or one of your friends help me with a problem? With Nelson's death, his pet store will be sold with any profits going to Milo when he turns eighteen, if he is proven innocent of killing his father. In the meantime, I have to deal with that pesky parrot, Feathers. No one seems to want him. I asked the school science teacher who said he was sorry, but he heard Feather's language at the pet store, and, frankly, it would not be acceptable language in a school.

"I tried Billy and Wayne at the bike shops, and they said that if he squawked as loudly as Feathers tends to do, he could pose a safety hazard since they both worked with sharp tools as they repair bikes and motorcycles. Deputy Murphy and I discussed keeping that impossible bird at the police station, but there would be privacy issues. If he repeated any names of victims or suspects, or any information about a crime, we could be held liable. Feathers does what all parrots do; he repeats what he hears sometimes. Can you help me out?"

"Well, I certainly can't keep him, pretty as he is. I

am constantly busy here at the bookshop and with my acting. I live in a small apartment by myself so there isn't anyone to help with his care. I am also sure my landlady would take offense at his language. Sorry, Sheriff, I wish I could help, but it's impossible."

I came up to the desk and joined in the conversation. "Feathers is a beautiful parrot, but his salty language would freak out the parents and be a bad influence for the children. I believe in vocabulary development, but not that kind of vocabulary. I also understand from Milo that Feathers is an expert at picking locks. Many a time, he has picked the lock on his cage and dive-bombed the employees and customers. One time he picked the lock on the back screen door that goes to the alley, and a customer spotted him flying in and out of a trash can looking for food and shiny objects."

Lola said, "I heard a report of this scene from Milo: Mr. Nelson heard a flustered customer scream, 'You need to capture that stupid bird before he attacks someone.' Then Mr. Nelson began screaming at his employees, 'You need to capture that menace before he attacks someone. How did he get out of the back door?' Of course, according to Milo, his dad blamed the poor kid for the escape."

I said, "Mark, I'm sorry, but no, I can't keep Feathers in my shop. He'd endanger the children, and if he picked the lock of his cage, he could damage my inventory."

"But, Robin, if I don't find someone to adopt that bird, he will have to be put to sleep. Feather is an exotic, rare, expensive, but feisty parrot. I also asked the zookeeper what to do, and he is searching for a zoo that might take him. He can't, but, hopefully, a home will become available soon. The problem is, meanwhile, where do I put Feathers until the zookeeper finds him a home?

"My other more vexing problem is what to do about Milo. If we find him innocent, as your Super Sleuths insist, where does he go? He's only fourteen. The Child Service's director says we need to turn him in to them."

"You can't do that," I said. "Surely someone in town can take him in. Sadie already has Billy living with her, and I have Asher and Mike living with me. Could you or Deputy Murphy take him in just temporarily until this whole murder mess is cleared up?"

"I don't think Child Services would allow it since we are both bachelors."

"I'll put in a call to all members of the Geezer Book Club. Maybe one of them would like to take Milo in to relieve their loneliness," I said. "Have you asked Omar Habbib? Ali is living with him but should soon have a job and will move out. Since Milo has been staying with him since you released him, Omar should know by now how Milo and Ahmram get along. He's a kind man and might be willing to give another kid a home. Meanwhile, I'll check with the others in the Geezer Book Club. Give me a few days to talk to them."

"Okay, I'll see if I can hold off the social worker for a week or so."

The sheriff headed out to the office.

Chapter 34

Schnoz Award

Billy was worried. He needed to get on with his plans, and these investigations of Wayne had derailed everything. He shoved aside all thoughts of murder and betrayal and was determined to examine his future. Billy asked Lola to meet with him. "I have a proposal that might be mutually beneficial. I can bring a picnic for breakfast in the park, and we can eat while we talk. You know me, always hungry."

"Why don't you just pick up some pastries from Sweet Indulgences," Lola said, "and come to my apartment instead? I'm not much of a cook, but I have one great recipe for scrambled eggs. I discovered it when they served it in the dining car on the Amtrak train to Los Angeles. This yummy recipe has eggs, chives, and diced ham. You'll love it. Come around eight or so."

Once the call ended, Billy felt giddy. *I've never been to Lola's apartment before. I hope she doesn't still see me as a kid. I turn eighteen next month and have been on my own since I was fourteen when my grandparents died. Because of my aunt's inheritance, I also own my own business even though I'm still seventeen for two more months. I'm just five years, two months, and three days younger than Lola, but who's counting? I want Lola to see me as an equal."*

Promptly at eight, hair properly mussed, and dressed in his best Motorcycle Repair Shop t-shirt, Billy rang the doorbell.

"Come on in."

Wow, Lola looks good even in a granny apron.

"Make yourself at home in the living room. I'm just putting the finishing touches on the eggs, then we can go on the deck to eat."

"Great, I'm starved."

Billy scanned the small living room and spotted a framed picture on the mantel. It showed a statue of a huge nose and a little girl in a fancy red dress. The caption read: The Schnoz Award, given to the youngest professional smeller in the perfume industry.

The deck was sunny and comfortable. When they sat down for breakfast at the round picnic table, Billy asked Lola about the award.

Lola explained to me, "My mom made money when I was about nine years old by shopping around her only daughter both as a perfumer, often called the nose or *nez* in French, and a taster because of my heightened sense of smell and taste. The perfume manufacturing companies were always looking to hire people to test out the smell of their new lines of perfumes and paid out good money for those with a heightened sense of smell."

"Does that mean you can smell normal things like garbage or cabbage more than others?"

"Yep, unfortunately, but on the positive side, I can even smell flowers like roses a block away."

"Did you love the job as a smeller?"

"Not really, but I understood that Mom encouraged

me because she needed the money."

"That doesn't sound very fair to you."

"Well, Mom wasn't about fairness. She didn't get much money from her singing engagements so I understood that she needed the money.

"The wine and beverage companies were also looking for tasters for their new beverages so until I was in high school, I would go into their manufacturing plants and test their new sodas and other beverages, all except the wine because I was too young. Mom usually was able to make her rent payments because of my nose.

"One night, the perfume companies hosted a banquet and gave out the SchnozAwards, named after a famous comedian from the seventies named Jimmy Durante. He often made fun of things nose-related. He answered to the nickname of the Schnoz because of his big nose and always signed off his performances with 'Goodnight, Mrs. Calabash, wherever you are.'

"Who cared who Mrs. Calabash was? As a kid, I thought that evening was ridiculous, but my mom saw it as an opportunity for a free meal and drinks. I wanted to turn invisible as I marched onto the stage to accept this stupid award. I kept it to remember my mom and my crazy messed up life." Lola paused a minute then said, "That's funny, Billy. I haven't shared that story with anyone before. Oh well, add it to your list of weird things you learn about people."

Billy laughed. "Good to know your secret talents. If I ever go to a fancy restaurant, I'll take you with me to choose the wine. Now, let me show you my suggested proposal.

"Wayne and I are having some serious

disagreements about running our repair shop and motorcycle showroom. I'm thinking about buying him out. If he agrees to the buyout, after graduation, I will consolidate the two businesses into one and operate them out of one large store. I'll put the repair shop in the large office space at the back of the showroom and a desk in a corner of the showroom to serve as a tiny open office to oversee all the paperwork with customers.

"If that goes well, since we own both buildings, I'll rent out the current repair shop to someone starting a new business. You would be first in line for consideration if you would like to consider this location for your acting studio. I know I can trust you to keep the store undamaged, and it would bring another creative business to Farley Square. We can talk about price, etc., and you can tell me how you want to use the space. Do you want it painted, divided into cubicles, etc.? I'm sure I could configure the space to your needs.

"I haven't told my plans to anyone else yet. The sheriff is checking out a few things about Wayne. I shake all over thinking of confronting him about buying him out. I feel like there's something fishy about him, and with all that's gone on with the shootings and murder of Nelson, I'm fearful that Wayne might have some connection to all the happenings. This might be an unfounded suspicion, but I'm trying to figure out some things. Please don't mention any of this conversation to anyone. We'll call it the secret Schnoz Conspiracy."

"I'll certainly keep this between us," Lola said. "I don't know Wayne well, but I'll snoop around a little. We've got time so let's meet again closer to graduation if you're successful in convincing Wayne to sell. Thanks for thinking of me, Billy. I would love to go ahead with my studio plans, and your shop sounds ideal, small enough, but also large enough for a small stage for acting, and smaller practice rooms."

"Lola, I need to get to school. Thanks for listening to my plans. I have a lot to

think about and what better place for thinking than sitting through Mr. Smith's boring history lesson.

****

Around noon, I received a frantic call from Sadie.

"Robin, you or Lola need to come to Sweet Indulgences right away. I tried to reach Sheriff Houtman or Deputy Murphy, but they are out on another case. I even tried Mr. Brump, but he didn't answer."

I interrupted her. "Mr. Brump will be here in about a half hour for the Geezer Book Club. Can this wait until then?"

"No, someone needs to come now. Please, hurry. No one is hurt yet."

I frantically told Lola the situation and left her in charge with instructions to tell Mr. Brump to head over as soon as he arrived.

I arrived at Sweet Indulgences in record time, burst through the door, and saw this amazing sight.

Cameron was grabbing his photographer, Andy, by the neck of his t-shirt and yelling at the top of his voice, "You traitor. I trust you with my personal information, and then I find out that you are going behind my back."

"Hang on, Cameron, what do you think I did?"

"Don't play innocent with me. First, you tell the sheriff lies about me, then I find out that you are starting your own business and abandoning me."

Andy sputtered, "Calm down. Calm down. Everyone is looking at us. Your nice guy reputation is going right down the drain. In an hour, you'll probably be banned from this town because, as I told you before, word spreads fast in a small town."

That sobered Cameron up a little. He looked around and realized that the twenty-some people in the coffee shop were staring at him and not in a friendly way. Cameron sat down and buried his face in his hands. He knew he needed to stop his drinking because he was prone to violent outbursts like now.

"Sadie," I said, "let me handle this. You try to mitigate the damage with your customers–maybe free cheesecake or something."

I slowly approached the two men. "Andy, why is this happening? You two are partners and have been for about three years. Why does Cameron think you are going behind his back?"

"If he would just listen to me, I could explain."

I gently touched Cameron on the shoulder. He jumped nervously. "What do you want? Butt out."

"Cameron, I can see and smell, I might add, that you have had more than enough to drink this early in the day. Are you ready to let Andy explain, or do I need to call the sheriff and have him haul you both into the jail to explain why you are disturbing a local business?"

The mention of the sheriff forced Cameron to look up and shake himself, trying to focus. At that moment, Mr. Brump appeared. "Do you need help, Sadie? Are these men bothering you?"

I spoke up. "Andy is just about to explain the cause of the misunderstanding between these two. We'd appreciate it, Mr. Brump, if you would witness their story since the sheriff is off on another case."

"That's what I am here for. Fire away."

Cameron haltingly began. "I-I heard that Andy took another job and was abandoning my videocast. We are contracted for this series, and I was warned by my producer that I must make a success of it or my career is finished. Andy is supposed to be my partner and my friend. I don't take well to people cheating on me and trying to damage my reputation."

"Andy, I think Cameron is ready to listen. Sit down here and explain yourself."

At first, the two men just glared at each other across the table. Finally, Andy asked, "I assume you heard about my ambitions from Lola?"

"Darn right I did and Billy also. They were walking down the street by the park in Pittman, and I was sitting on a bench, just observing the town folk talking and walking. Billy was gushing about renting his store to Lola or maybe to you to start a photography store. What was I supposed to think? This was the first I heard of you going off on your own."

"I did speak to Lola about my dream of becoming an independent photographer, but we never discussed opening my own shop here in Pittman. Lola tends to be enthusiastic and quick to act on ideas. This was all on her.

"Now that the idea is out there, we do need to talk about my future plans, but not when you're in such a foul mood, to put it mildly. You need to realize that your behavior affects not only your reputation, but mine also. Let's sit down on Friday when we are editing the footage for the videocast. Meet me here about six p.m., and don't drink before you come. If you appear here drunk again, that's the end of our contract. Ms. George and Sadie, would you please join us? Mr. Brump, thanks for coming. We didn't mean to cause such a ruckus."

Andy continued. "Thanks, Ms. George, for intervening in our dispute. We owe you."

Cameron just hung his head and looked longingly at Sadie hoping for some sympathy, but she gave him a hardened stare. Abruptly, he stood up and left the store.

Andy, Sadie, Mr. Brump, and I just watched him leave with no desire to follow him. *We probably should relate this incident to Sheriff Houtman,* I thought.

Chapter 35

Nostalgia

When I went back to my bookstore, I thought, *Maybe, I do need to get out of town for a while. All of this tension is getting to me.*

Matt Clare moved here just before school started, enrolled the boys at the high school, and signed them up for band. Asher and Mike took them under their wings so they would feel comfortable starting a new school. Matt liked the house I found, and now they are comfortably settled. He's been trying to convince me to return home with him to Kentucky during the kids' winter break for a visit as he tries to convince investors to finance his Children's Theater project in Pittman.

I'm running out of excuses. Asher and Mike will want to ski over break because all the ski teams rev up at that time. Both of them are racing, and they need some time to practice on the slopes. I could leave them in Marie's care since I won't see much of them when they spend their days at the ski slopes.

I decided to write a list to try to make an objective decision. This is my usual way of approaching decisions in complicated situations.

PRO

—I'd get to spend more time with Matt.

—It's been 3 years since I've seen my former

home and many friends.

—Paula will be thrilled to have me stay with them and catch up on our lives.

—I could forget about thieves and killers.

—I would feel safe.

—It would be nice to have someone wine and dine me at my former home.

CON

—I'm happy with spending time in my bookstore.

—I have no desire to be involved with the Children's Theater.

—I'll support Matt, but I have my own business to run.

—What if Asher or Mike get hurt while skiing?

—How would Sadie handle all the problems with Mr. H, Ali, Cameron, and Sheriff Houtman? Sadie needs me.

—What about Lola and her problems?

-Too many people are counting on me.

As I gazed at the list of pros and cons, I realized there wasn't a clear-cut easy decision.

The pros and cons were about equal. I pondered what other factors could influence my decision.

OTHER FACTORS

—A longing for love again

—Asher's need for a man's influence in his life

—Would too many memories of my John come flooding back when I returned to Kentucky?

—Would these memories overwhelm me with sadness and make me feel guilty for even considering another chance at romance?

—Does Pittman and its residents need me to keep residents of the town safe?

I need someone objective as a sounding board, someone removed from the action, but who? Maybe, Marie, who would be intuitive enough to see the conflict that could arise between Lola and Sadie. Marie is a wise lady who has had many experiences in life and has learned from those experiences. She learned to analyze problems, without jumping to conclusions. Marie also is honest and will not shield me from what I don't want to hear. Age has its benefits.

I think I will invite Marie over for dinner tomorrow night while the boys are at band practice, and she can help me make a responsible decision.

****

The next night, when Marie came over for supper, I jumped right in and said, "I need your help with a decision. You know about my friend, Matt Clare, who came to visit from my hometown in Kentucky and now lives here. He thinks I need a break from all the stress lately in our town. Matt has proposed that I go back to Kentucky with him for a few days this winter, leaving the bookstore in Lola and Edna Mae's capable hands. Do you think you could stay here with Asher and Mike since they are on the ski team? I know you get up early to go to the bakery, but they are quite able to get up and to the ski slopes in time. I am only worried about dinner and supervision on the nights they return early from ski team practice."

Marie listened to my pros and cons. Then I showed her the list of the other factors. "Let's have dessert while I ponder your dilemma."

After eating Marie's scrumptious blueberry cobbler, she put down her fork and said, "I understand Matt's concerns, plus he seems to have your best interests at heart. Visualize what you would be thinking about while you are in Kentucky. Would you be able to relax? Or would you instead be worried about the murder, the shooter, the boys, Sadie, graduation plans, choosing a college for Asher, etc.?

"Though I would be glad to stay with the boys, I don't think this plan is your best way of mitigating your stress. I think your time would be better spent listing and then addressing each of your concerns by staying right here in Pittman. Prioritize that list, then assign a certain amount of time each day to deal with each problem. So far, you have been approaching each problem as it occurred, then piling that problem on top of the others, and that builds up stress.

"I don't think that running away is the answer, enticing as it sounds. You need to make your life here more manageable. If you explain your need for priorities to Matt, assure him that after graduation things should slow down, and suggest that then you two can spend some quality time together, either in Kentucky, Pittman, or some cabin in the mountains. He should understand if he truly cares about having a relationship with you, or even if he just wants to be your friend."

At first, I felt deflated. I really wanted to go with Matt. His concern for my welfare was a plus in our relationship, but then, although disappointed not to go home to Kentucky and spend some time with old friends, I felt relieved.

"Marie, I value your experienced consideration of my problem. Thank you." I gave her a big hug thinking back to my teen years when my mother gave me such good advice that I've treasured all my life. I miss her hugs, but it's good to have a huggable friend like Marie.

She patted me on my back. "Now, you need to get some quality sleep. The boys should be home soon from band. Give them each a hug and explain that you are worn out and need to turn in early. Say goodnight and tell them you will listen to whatever they have to say at breakfast."

With that advice, this wise woman left me to ponder her advice.

****

I got up at six, and after a soothing shower, I felt like a new woman. When I approached the kitchen, I smelled bacon and pancakes cooking. *Uh, oh,* I thought, *I wonder what's up?*

Mike and Asher triumphantly smiled at me.

"Mom," said Asher, "we need to fill you in on what we have learned. Please don't comment until we finish so we can get everything in before we have to leave for school.

"Billy has fallen in love with Feathers, and he plans to train Feathers to greet customers with a hi and a peppy dance, and he will keep him in his Repair Shop. That way, Feathers can't do any harm since Billy is quite capable of designing a parrot-proof lock on Feathers' cage."

I didn't say a word, but I couldn't help laughing as I visualized Billy's training sessions with Feathers.

"We think Billy has a crush on Lola since she invited him to her apartment recently."

I stared at the boys in shock, but Asher put up his hand and said, "Next."

"Cameron and Andy, his photographer, had an argument at their taping of the dancing troupe from

Japan in the town square. We're not sure what the confrontation was about, but they both had red faces and looked about to tear into each other. Fortunately, Deputy Murphy and Mr. Brump were walking together to the coffee shop and stopped to see if they needed to intervene in the squabble. When the two men spotted the deputy and former detective, they both stomped away in opposite directions, leaving the dance troupe bewildered as to what had taken place."

It's been a busy day for two teenagers who were just walking to and from band practice, I thought.

Mike said, "Since the mellophones and saxophones were excused from practicing yesterday, I was eating my sack dinner in the Pittman Forest last night for a break before I came home to hit the books and finish my piles of homework. I spotted Cameron and Wayne huddled together and whispering. What do you suppose they were conspiring about? I didn't think they even knew each other very well."

I had no idea so I just shook my head.

As I finished my tasty breakfast, I realized it was already time for the boys to catch the bus, and I needed to touch base with Sadie before going to work. The boys were right. We don't have time to discuss all of this now.

"What time do the two of you get home tonight?"

Mike said, "I won't be home until about nine-thirty. Mr. Habbib wants to talk to me about his plan to possibly run Ten Pins until my dad is out of prison. I'm going over to his house after band practice tonight if that's okay with you?"

Asher said, "I'll be home by seven thirty because it's a shortened practice tonight."

"You know I don't like you boys walking home alone with a murderer running around our town. Mike, I also don't want you wandering around the Pittman Forest. Mike, Asher, and I will pick you up at Mr. Habbib's's house. Asher, I will pick you up at band practice, and we can get some dinner before Mike is ready."

"But, Mom."

"But, Ms. George."

"No buts. You two need to realize how dangerous things are right now until the sheriff finds Nelson's killer and the sniper at Tanglewood. I don't plan to lose either of you to violence. Sadie has even taken to carrying a gun, which worries me."

Both boys realized from my tone of voice the gravity of the situation.

"Okay, I'll wait in front of school, Mom."

"If you text me, Mike, when you're finished at Mr. Habbib's, we will come to pick you up."

"I'll be waiting on his porch," said Mike.

Chapter 36

A Job Not Finished

Early in the morning, the contractor and the second hitman met again in Pittman Forest. Shaded by trees, no one could see them.

The killer was getting anxious.

The scary contractor was getting impatient. He menacingly said, "You assured me that you were up to all three assignments, but now you seem to be faltering and getting cold feet. Aresh suggested you would be a good replacement for that coward we hired at first. I fired him, and his life won't be worth a dime when the vengeful terrorists find him. Aresh said you were capable of the job since you had accomplished several hits successfully for his friends. Your reputation is impressive. I warned you when I hired you on Aresh's recommendation that I expected complete loyalty, or else.

"You promised to deliver. I hired you to kill my money launderer because he is skimming money from my profits. I heard that Nelson was dead, but can you prove that you were the one who killed him?"

"Yes, and I have a photo to prove that Nelson, your cheating mark, is indeed dead. This photo should prove to you and Aresh that I am capable of carrying out the next two assignments. First, though, I need you to pay me now for killing Nelson. Then I will get to Aresh's assignments."

"Your money will turn up in your account as soon as I discretely verify the kill with law enforcement.

"Aresh is getting tired of waiting. When he found out about Nelson's murder, Aresh accused me of interfering with his contract with you. Now, he's accused me of being less than loyal by stealing his hitman even though he was the one who recommended you. I don't want to be on the bad side of an unreasonable man like Aresh."

"Okay, okay, I understand. Do you think I am stupid? The other two assassinations are just proving more complicated. The victims are well-known and loved in Pittman. I must find a way to do this discreetly, so I don't get caught. The first assassin you hired attempted the hit at Tanglewood, but failed, so you decided to pay me to kill Nelson, and Aresh hired me to kill his two targets. I set your assignment as well as Aresh's in motion. I succeeded with your kill, and I am working on a plan to complete Aresh's assignment."

"Well, you better work faster. I will give you two weeks. If Aresh's assignment is not finished by then, you will not get paid, and I warn you if I don't kill you, my boss will, and you don't want to mess with him.

"You're in the big leagues now where the real money is, but along with the huge payouts comes greater risk. Your fear of discovery may be well founded, but your fear of dying should be what is motivating you. Remember, two weeks."

With that threat, the would-be executioner exited the forest.

Shaking, I collapsed on the soft grass by the picnic

table and stared at the cloudy sky. *What am I going to do? Being a hired hitman had sounded like a financially rewarding occupation. I suffered so much abuse as a child, I have no feelings of remorse when I inflict pain on others. I don't think kindness or remorse are in my DNA.*

Resolving to come up with a new plan, the hitman left the forest with resolve. Kill, collect my money, flee, and disappear escaping small town living forever.

Maybe I'll leave the country, buy a bungalow on a beach, and become a beach bum. That would be the life. For any future assignments, the contractors can just contact me on the beach.

I closed my eyes and began to dream about my financially independent future.

Chapter 37

Controversies

Our peaceful town has been transformed by controversies.

The eight regulars in the Geezer Book Club gathered at the Bookworm Shop for their monthly meeting. Edna Mae started the session with a short clip from an old-fashioned western that had cowboys hidden behind huge rocks, shooting six shooters and rifles. This seemed appropriate since the topic of discussion this week was how firearms were depicted in books, from the old shoot 'em up westerns to the more modern books about hunters and the hunted.

Easygoing Beth was the peacemaker, and though several members protested the choice of this topic, she reminded them that history often repeats itself, and if more people were well-read, they might not replicate the same mistakes made in history. A well-read person would be better equipped to handle such controversies as the recent debate going on about gun ownership or a ban on guns.

Mr. Brump, drawing on his prior occupation as a detective, mirrored his name as the resident Grump. "I must strongly defend a person's right to own a gun, but I firmly object to people owning the kind of machine guns and rifles available today. A gun for protection, yes. A gun for hunting, yes, but any other use of a gun only becomes dangerous for others."

Marie turned to Mr. Brump and said, "Surely though, there have to be restrictions on certain kinds of firearms, and there must be rules on who can own a gun."

Harley, debonair and an intellectual, often contributed an elegant viewpoint to all discussions. This time, he asked, "What kinds of registration rules are in place in Massachusetts?"

Bart, the researcher and teacher, rattled off the restrictions on owning guns. Mr. Brump protested. "There are so many illegal guns that have never been registered. Why I've arrested teenagers that could in no way have gotten the gun legally that they used to murder and commit robbery."

Gramps jumped into the heated discussion. "I think the main problem is that our youth in this area are not engaged in healthy activities to keep them out of trouble. I blame the city commissioners for not providing enough lawful and interesting activities for our youth."

"I object to that," said Edna Mae. "Look at all the youth are offered through the schools—band, football, basketball, tennis, and soccer. The city commissioners are not their parents. Parents have an obligation to see how their teenagers spend their time."

Lola added, "We have an active theater scene with classes for any kids who are interested in music or acting, even dance."

'But don't you think the city leaders could do more?"

"What else do you want them to do, Gramps? My

boys are totally involved in after-school and summer activities. They barely have time for schoolwork," I added to their discussion.

Harley said, "Robin, that's because your son and Mike, your foster son, know what you expect, and know what rules you expect them to follow. Not all parents are that clear, so they, not the commissioners, are responsible for knowing about their kids' actions. Gangs wouldn't exist if not for parental neglect."

After about an hour of back and forth, Mr. Brump stood up and abruptly headed to the door shouting, "You opinionated, stubborn, egotists, you have no idea of how to carry on a discussion without making people who don't agree with you feel shamed and guilty for having their strong ideas. I've had it. I bet none of you have ever fired a gun or needed to fire one. You've never encountered a gang or understood that they often fill a void in a teen's life as they seek a place to belong." Out Mr. Brump stomped.

Edna Mae wisely called for the meeting to adjourn before anyone else could display animosity to any others in our book club.

Later, as I was relaying this incident to Sadie, we began to reminisce.

Sadie told the story of joining the Resistance Movement in her village and scrounging around to find enough guns to form a formidable defense of her village. "We met twice a week in various hidden locations to perfect our prowess with guns. If we weren't good shots, we wouldn't stay alive very long. Guns were essential to our safety and the safety of the whole village."

I said, "I think everyone in the book club would

have a tough time relating to that survival need except Mr. Brump, who had to deal with criminals. I led a very sheltered life in Kentucky. Yes, most rural Kentuckians owned guns, but they were for hunting, hunting for sport, and hunting to eat. Gangs, who threatened citizens with their guns, were practically nonexistent except in recent years in the larger cities."

"I think Mr. Brump is right," Sadie said. "We won't get anywhere with the gun controversy until we learn to be respectful of each person's point of view."

"Who knew such an interesting topic as guns in literature could cause such controversy," I said. "I do have one request, Sadie. Since I know you carry a gun, I urge you to be very careful. I don't want anything to happen to my best friend."

"Don't worry, Robin, I'm an expert shot."

That's what I am worried about.

Chapter 38

Scene at Sweet Indulgences

Matt and Lola were deep in discussion. "Why do you want to know about the incident at Tanglewood?" asked Lola.

"I've been a director and producer in Chicago and Cincinnati, and I'm thinking of investing in a new Children's Theater here in Pittman," Matt said. "It will alternately cater to an adult group interested in improv comedy as well as children. I talked to Robin about this, and she was all for the idea. Since you are an actress, I wondered what you would think of this idea. I can't build here unless I think it is a safe community for children. At Second City, adult improv has been so successful over the years in Chicago, and even their road shows have been well attended. I think the Berkshires are ready for this type of fun. However, crime is spiking here as the recent murder of Horatio Nelson proves. I may have to rethink this. The relatively safe environment of this small town is essential to achieving success."

"I agree, Matt," Lola said. "A children's theater is needed. It would provide opportunities for teens and younger children to be involved in creative activities. They will then have less time to commit the random acts of vandalism being promoted by some gangs to our middle and high school kids.

"The other day, many of the shops on Farley Square had their windows smashed, and paint was splashed on the doors of shops. There is an undercurrent of animosity and some drug use among the teens in particular. There also is a fair amount of prejudice against any ethnic groups. Mr. Habbib was shocked when he first moved here that some people had torn up his lawn and trashed his lawn furniture. They didn't go quite as far as when Sadie first came to Pitman, and that evil man, Mopey Tyler, wrote on Sadie's restaurant walls, 'Foreigners Not Welcome Here' and 'Go Home Where You Belong.'

"Shakespeare and Company in Stockbridge and The Berkshire Museum in Pittman have sponsored classes for children this fall and winter, hoping to give them a safe environment for their creativity. They have been working on making the children realize that prejudice against others is wrong. Kids of all ethnic groups, both tourists and town people, participate and learn that everyone can work together and respect each other."

"Lola, maybe you and I can find a way to partner and share our love of theater with these children."

"I will certainly think about that. I'm currently mapping out my future plans, and one of the plans includes opening an acting center where I give acting lessons to the community and put on community plays. Let's see how your plans might jive with mine. But I also agree that these crimes must be solved."

"Lola, keep me apprised of any progress you make. Feel free to contact me by phone or email to run any ideas or questions by me. We would make a great team,

I think. I'm liking this town more and more each day. I'm glad I moved here."

****

Omar Habbib was grateful that the sheriff cleared him of Nelson's murder. The kids he took out for Halloween had all vouched for him to the sheriff.

Mr. Habbib's thoughts were focused on the future and Sam's offer to run Ten Pins.

Omar looked out the window and saw Ahmram outside running around the driveway shooting hoops and getting rid of his excessive energy.

Ahmram has thrived since we came to Pittman last year. In second grade now, his English has greatly improved, and he almost sounds like a native. I hope that my career plans won't have a negative effect on him.

Omar shouted out the window, "Time to go to Sadie's barbeque. Come in and get ready. You're in charge of carrying the cupcakes."

Ahmram bounced into the house and went to clean up, then grabbed the cupcakes we had purchased at Marie's bakery.

"I'm ready, Dad. I'll take the cupcakes to the car."

I wish his mom were here to see what a great kid her son has become.

****

When Habbib arrived at Sadie's monthly barbeque, most of the people were already filling their plates with hummus, pita tacos stuffed with fried ground lamb with onions and pine nuts topped with tahini sauce. Numerous salads, and yummy desserts filled the table. Mike and Asher were manning the grill with Bart O'Neal from the Geezer Book Club. They were cooking vegetables, hamburgers, and veggie burgers, and Bart was making his famous ribs. No one will ever go home hungry from Sadie's barbeques.

Omar went over to a long table where I was sitting with the Super Sleuths, and the Geezer Book Club members were digging into their piled-high plates. He asked for their input on a deal he was thinking of accepting.

He began, "Sam, Mike's dad, has offered me a limited partnership in Ten Pins Bowling Alley, thanks to Mike's recommendation. I would like to run the terms by you to see if you think this is reasonable. My brother will go over the terms and draw up the necessary legal documents.

"The profits will be split seventy/thirty. Seventy percent will cover expenses and my salary, and the other thirty percent will go into a bank account for Mike. The initial expenses for supplies, etc. to get the business restarted will come from the business account being held at the bank in Mike's name.

"I have two fears. One, I don't want to disrupt Ahmram's routines, but I think I've solved that problem. Gramps has agreed to come to our house and babysit so Ahmram can be in his own home and not have to go to after-school care. He will be there when my son gets home from school, fix him dinner, and tuck him into bed at night.

Gramps said, "I look on all these boys as the grandsons I never had, so I'll be glad to spend some time with him. Not only will this help you, but it will be a comfort to me."

"If Gramps can't be there some days, I will set up a mattress in the back office, and I can watch him there.

Since this partnership isn't a long-term contract, I will have time to evaluate if there is any negative effect on my son.

"Two other negatives I'd like to mention. When Sam gets out of prison, he and I might not get along. I've never met him. And two, if we don't hit it off, I will have spent a year or two in someone else's business without developing my own business."

The Super Sleuths and Geezers were quick to comment.

Sadie said, "The sheriff seems to be getting closer to finding the motive for the shooting. He told me last night when he stopped in Sweet Indulgences that they had narrowed down the suspect list to three. He did say he cleared Milo."

Lola said, "Everyone keeps saying 'he or she.' Surely, the sheriff doesn't suspect a woman. Could he be wrong again and suspect me, or Robin, or Sadie? Oh, that man makes me nervous."

Mike, holding a plate with a huge, juicy hamburger on it, joined the group. "You all look so serious. What's going on?"

I told Mike, "Mr. Habbib is considering taking up Sam on his offer of a limited partnership and was asking for our input."

At first, Mike tensed and glared angrily at Mr. Habbib and the whole group. "Mr. Habbib, you do realize that I haven't even heard from Dad except that one time he proposed to offer you the partnership, and I told him I thought you would do a good job. That phone call ended with me, accusing my dad of abandoning me because he hadn't even written an answer to any of my letters. He also never called me even on Christmas or my birthday. Some father he is. Good luck, Mr. Habbib, but don't expect too much support from my unconcerned dad."

Mike was positively fuming when he said, "When Dad leaves prison and returns to Pittman, I'm out of here and going as far away as possible."

Mike went back to the grill and took his anger out on the remaining burgers.

Asher stood by Mike at the grill and tried to calm him down, but that was a fruitless effort. Those poor hamburgers were smushed and redefined the definition of charred burgers.

The sheriff and Deputy Murphy entered the backyard and observed Mike's reaction to whatever was being discussed. Mark Houtman said to his deputy, "I didn't realize that Mike had such a temper, did you?"

Murphy said, "You don't suppose we should consider Mike for the death of Nelson since it looks like a death caused by passion? Maybe we need to expand our list of suspects."

Just then, Billy and Wayne arrived carrying packs of cold drinks and a couple of snack bags. Wayne looked extremely uncomfortable, but he hadn't been around lately and had missed several of the monthly get-togethers. He could also be a little embarrassed about ignoring the neighborhood group.

I watched them head to the picnic table while I questioned the sheriff." I said, "We are very afraid that Cameron Coldren and Andy are either going to back out of doing the video cast or change the focus to one of the crimes in small towns that would negatively reflect on our town and ruin our tourist trade. If you can solve the crimes, we might save the reputation of our town."

"Why aren't they here?" asked Murphy.

I said, "We're not sure, but we're worried. Our tourists are vital to the success of our merchants. We threatened Cameron about canceling the agreement, but he just said that we sealed the agreement with only a handshake, and he couldn't be held to it. We're checking with our lawyer to see how binding a handshake is."

Deputy Murphy asked, "Has anyone seen either of these men recently?"

Sadie said, "Not since yesterday when Robin and I confronted them and told them that the community agreed to have them do the video cast because we were sure they would report on the positive aspects of small-town living, not the negatives."

Sheriff Houtman said, "I think it's time I checked these guys out more thoroughly. We did a cursory search into Cameron Coldren's background, but we only found information for the last four years, nothing before that. I'll let you know if I find anything suspicious.

Chapter 39

Another Secret Meeting

Lola decided to do some of her own detective work. She and the others were shocked to see Mike's temper flare up at the barbeque. She thought that might make the sheriff suspect that Mike was violent enough to kill Nelson. The sheriff also considered Andy or Cameron suspects, not only for Nelson's murder but also for the shooting at Tanglewood. Lola considered these accusations preposterous but hesitated to say anything because the next thing she could expect to happen would be that the inept sheriff would accuse her, and her suitor, Robert Murphy, would be too wimpy to disagree with his boss.

It's up to me to disprove these theories. I need to talk to Andy. I intend to figure out who is responsible for Nelson's murder.

Lola called Andy. "I absolutely need to see you today, Andy. Can you meet me this evening?"

"Sure, Lola, how about I take you to dinner and we can talk?"

"No, that won't work. This meeting must be secret. How about picking up some Chinese food or a pizza and bringing it to my apartment? I should be home by seven-thirty. I'll text you the address."

Once Lola settled this, she needed a plan to present

to Andy.

****

The next morning, I found Lola, sitting at the cash register, lost in contemplation. She jumped when I came up to the counter. "Relax, Lola. You seemed lost in thought so I didn't want to startle you. Is anything wrong?"

"How about my whole life?"

"Lola, you need to talk to me or someone. Please tell me what is so horrible in your life to create this much anxiety?"

"Oh, Robin, I wish I could just pour my heart out, but it's too broken. I need to decide my future. I thought opening the acting studio was a perfect plan, but now things have happened to change those plans. These crimes need to be solved so I can get on with my own life."

"Has someone threatened you, or are you scared of something? Most of the town is in a state of fear because the sheriff hasn't caught the perpetrator. You could just be a victim of crowd frenzy."

"Robin," Lola burst out, "the sheriff might suspect Andy, and, and, I think I'm falling in love with him. We were discussing Andy's plans the other day to pursue a photography opportunity that has been offered to him working at a travel magazine in New York.

"I've also been offered an opportunity in New York. A producer, who saw me in the performance of *The Taming of the Shrew* at Shakespeare and Company, wants me to audition for an off-Broadway play. Agatha Christie's book, *A Pocket Full of Rye*, is being adapted into a play with one major innovation. A female will play Scotland Yard Detective Inspector Neele, not a male. This opens so many new directions for the play to go. Instead of the typical English detective, I will create a brand-new character, the first female inspector at Scotland Yard who will partner with Miss Marple, who could be played by Lily Tomlin. That will create an entirely new perspective on their roles. I would love to be in a play with someone as famous as Ms. Tomlin. I admire her acting ability so very much. Can't you just picture her as Miss Marple?"

I said, "That would be amazing. I can also think of other talented artists who I've often pictured as Ms. Marple. No matter who is picked, I'm sure the uniqueness of a female inspector could carry the show. How sure is it that you will get the part?"

"I'm fairly sure the producer wants me unless I blow the audition. I've been putting my time into intensely practicing my scene. This is my chance to break into the big time as an actress."

"But what about your future dreams of opening an acting studio? Also, what about the partnership you discussed with Matt about the Children's Theater in Pittman?"

"I am going to put those on hold. I can always try again when I've accomplished my dream of becoming a famous actress.

"I must ask a favor. I need to take off work Monday and Tuesday, maybe even Wednesday if I have to wait for callbacks. The audition is set for Tuesday morning in New York. Is that okay with you, Robin?"

"Of course. Who am I to stand in the way of your fame?"

"In the meantime, it is imperative that we clear Andy's name. Who do you think the murderer and the hitman at Tanglewood are? And who is behind this whole plot? Certainly not Andy, but who? I'm still a little suspicious of Cameron. He acts incredibly nervous, especially when he is near the sheriff or Mr. Brump. He also seemed quite cross with Andy and Wayne the other day. He's a smart man. Could he be behind organizing these crimes?"

"I'm as perplexed as you and the sheriff are. We need to find a brilliant schemer who has a motive. So far, I'm not satisfied with the sheriff's conclusions, but the Super Sleuths are at an impasse. Sadie and I are meeting with them again tonight. You might want to join us."

Chapter 40

Take a Shot

Asher ran onto Sadie's porch just before the other Super Sleuths arrived and waved a flyer in the air. "The rumor is true," he gasped, "Mr. and Mrs. Stanley are moving to Florida and have sold Stanley's Hardware to Barney Barton who is turning it into a gun shop with a shooting range in the rear courtyard. They've already stocked the store and are about to open. Barney will name it BB's Take a Shot. Do you think I can go to the shooting range, Mom?"

I just stared at my growing teenage son. "Maybe, we'll see."

Well, you can imagine that this is not the town's first choice for a new shop in Farley Square. "Of all the cute boutiques that could have moved into that prime retail space, why would the Stanleys sell to someone who wants to promote gun ownership?" I asked Sadie.

"I think it is a splendid idea for a shop," said Sadie. "I talked to Mrs. Stanley a few weeks ago, and she asked me not to say anything yet. They felt gun training was needed in the town, so they sold their store to a nephew who is a gun activist. Many people around here go hunting for deer and rabbits. I'd rather have them take a proper class in shooting than just be handed a rifle by their dad or grandpa, who takes them on their first hunting trip, and just says, 'You just point and shoot.'"

I said, "I don't necessarily agree with you, Sadie. Yes, kids learn to hunt from their dads or grandpas, but those relatives, I'm sure stress the need for safety and responsibility. I don't think a store training people to shoot guns would have prevented the shooter at Tanglewood. How can we trust that the wrong people won't get their hands on a firearm? Surely, no one's dad or grandpa would hand a rifle to the next generation and say, 'Go out and try to kill someone.'"

Sadie disagreed with me about the gun shop. "I guess we'll get the community's point of view as soon as word spreads about this new store."

Asher spoke up. "I can tell you what the teens think. BB's Take a Shot will have a line out the door when they open for lessons and target practice sessions."

"That's all we need in our town just now as everyone is dealing with their fears of murders and mayhem hitting home," I said.

When the Super Sleuths arrived, we ran the idea of a gun shop by them. They were split fifty-fifty. I sighed. "We mimic the rest of the country. Some see the value of owning guns and having a prominent gun shop where guns are readily available. The rest think it is a good idea for families to own and learn how to use guns properly. Let's solve the shooting at Tanglewood. Then I might be more open to a gun shop here in our town."

The next morning about noon, I was about to take a break for lunch when I looked out my shop window and saw a mob of people marching around Farley Square, holding signs saying, STOP THE GUNS and NO GUN SHOP NEEDED HERE. On the opposite side of the street was a line of people with opposing signs: PROTECT OUR SECOND AMENDMENT RIGHTS, POWER TO THE PEOPLE, and QUIT STOMPING ON OUR GUNS. Both lines of marchers seemed to have about equal numbers. It looks like our town is split right down the middle on the gun issue. I wonder where Sheriff Houtman and Deputy Murphy are.

My phone rang. "Yes, Sadie?"

"Robin, have you seen the protesters?"

"Of course. Sit tight. I don't want you or any of the kids involved in this march. Someone could get hurt if it turns violent. We're responsible for the boys. Hopefully, they are at school and aren't aware of what's going on."

Just then, I spotted many of the band members, including Asher and Mike in the march supporting the Second Amendment rights.

"Do you see Billy?" Sadie asked.

"Yes, he's standing outside his shop with Wayne. No signs or anything, just staring."

Later that night, under cover of darkness, a gang of anti-gun advocates broke windows gaining access to the inventory in the gun shop. They stole many guns and proceeded to march down Rt. 7 to Smith's Farm where they built a bonfire to melt down the guns.

Sheriff Houtman and Deputy Murphy were called by some concerned citizens who witnessed the building of the bonfire and were afraid it would spread to neighboring fields.

By the time the sheriff and deputy arrived, the culprits had taken off and thrown water and sand on the bonfire to extinguish it. Another mystery for our overworked lawmen to solve!

When the boys came in from band, I warned them that I better not find out that they were involved in the theft and bonfire. Both Asher and Mike denied any involvement and assured me their friends also were not involved. If anything, they were pro-guns, not building bonfires to melt them.

"I hope you are telling me the truth. If not, you will never set foot in that gun shop, lessons or not."

****

Gramps, Omar Habbib, and Ali were eating dinner and talking about the shooting at Tanglewood. Mr. H said to Ali, "You've told us that you were involved in the sniper attack. Now, you must go to the sheriff and tell him what happened at Tanglewood."

Ali put down his fork. He couldn't eat another bite. His stomach was clenching, and he started to tap his fingers on the table. "I can't. You don't know about a phone call I had with Aresh, the ISIS leader who hired me and gave me instructions on whom to kill and how.

"He threatened me. Aresh said, 'I will find you, coward, and I or one of my hitmen will eliminate you. You don't have long to live so it's time to get your affairs in order. You won't see us coming. See you soon, coward.'

"If you make me go to the sheriff, and he puts me in jail, I will be a sitting target for the killers. I need to flee tonight."

"Where will you go?"

"I have no clue, and if I did, I wouldn't tell you because they would consider you an accomplice in my disappearance and would have no hesitancy in eliminating you and your friends and family."

Ahmram at eight-years-old understood part of what the two grownups were talking about. He spoke up. "Ali, you can't leave us. You promised to come to our school for Sports Day tomorrow. You were going to be my partner in the three-legged race, and you agreed to be a ref in the soccer game. Please, Ali, don't leave me."

Ahmram got up from the table, climbed up on Ali's lap, and wrapped him in a tight hug. Ali could hardly catch his breath. He was overwhelmed by Ahmram's love and his clinging and sobbing. *How can I break this boy's heart, but I must if I'm going to survive.*

Mr. H and Gramps watched this drama unfold and decided they needed to step in and help Ali make his decision. "Ali, if you want to spend the rest of your life running from these killers, and constantly looking over your shoulder for assassins, you are an adult and can make your own choices, and I can't stop you, but there is another path."

Ali looked at Mr. H in disbelief. "What other choices are there?"

Gramps said, "You are now part of our Pittman family, Ali. We will help the sheriff see the wisdom of releasing you into our custody. We will protect you."

Mr. H said, "Gramps, will you stay with Ahmram, and I will accompany Ali to the sheriff's office. I can call him now and tell him we need to see him about the incident at Tanglewood. I will also demand that he promises not to put you in jail, and you will tell him everything and help to prevent another assassination of someone very dear to him. I'm sure the sheriff will agree to these terms."

A half-hour later, Mr. H and Ali walked into the office. Sheriff Houtman and Deputy Murphy were there. "Sit down, please," said the sheriff. "I'm going to ask you questions, Ali, and I'm going to record our conversation. Do you agree?"

"Yes, sheriff." Ali, shoulders bent and head hanging low, sat down to answer the sheriff's questions. Mr. H informed the sheriff that he would be present and wouldn't leave Ali's side.

"Okay."

"How are you involved in the shooting at Tanglewood?"

"I was the shooter. I raised my rifle, sited my targets, and deliberately missed my targets."

"Who were your targets?"

"Sadie and Omar Habbib."

Shocked, the sheriff said, "Sadie and Mr. Habbib? Why would you attempt to shoot Sadie?"

"At this point in my life, I was a brainwashed terrorist. Aresh, our leader, gave me orders to assassinate Sadie because she was a member of the Resistance in our town." Ali looked guiltily at Mr. Habbib. "This is the first that Mr. H has heard that he also was a target because he was in the Resistance. Aresh and his followers were tracking down all Resistance fighters who had fled the country. He promised me a lot of money and an esteemed position as one of his many hitmen if I completed this mission successfully.

"I came to the Boston airport and met up with my ISIS handler in the USA. He came to my hotel room, gave me the rifle and some other guns as well as a new identity." He repeated Aresh's instructions.

"Since I was out of the clutches of ISIS, I thought about Sadie, her brother, Alex, and you, Omar. As boys, we had all always been great friends. Now, I was supposed to kill my friend's sister who always looked up to me just like she looked up to her older brother. I also thought of how kind you have been to me, welcoming me into your family. Ahmram looks up to me like an older brother. What was I thinking? Had I completely given up my moral compass? What was I becoming?"

"What did this contact look like?" asked the sheriff.

"When I heard the knock on my hotel room door, I opened it to this man in disguise. He said that Aresh recommended me as a reliable hitman. The contractor said, 'I also have a personal assignment for you. I would like to commission you to kill a person who is supposed to be laundering my drug money profits. To eliminate this man, I am willing to pay you many thousands of dollars. If you agree to kill this cheater and accomplish the assignment, I will recommend you as a hitman for the Northeastern United States. This would be very lucrative for you and would guarantee your financial future. If, however, you fail, your life will not be worth much because I will track you down and kill you.'

"I was petrified. At that moment, I realized how much I had transformed from a person with a justifiable cause to a radical terrorist. I couldn't stand myself and what I had become."

"What did the man look like?" the sheriff repeated.

"I couldn't identify him. He had on a beige trench coat and a hat pulled down over his face. He sported sunglasses and a scarf masking most of his face, and he disguised his voice."

"Do you think you could identify him now?"

"No. He contacted me again after I botched the hit on Sadie at Tanglewood. He relayed Aersh's threat. If I didn't accomplish this hit on Sadie and Omar, Aresh would seek revenge. I didn't care. I told him to tell Aresh to find a new hitman."

"How did the man react to this?"

"He stormed out of the room warning me that my days are numbered."

"Do you know who he got to replace you as a hitman?"

"No."

"So you are saying that Aresh is sending a new hitman to kill Sadie and Mr. H, and the drug lord is sending a new hitman to kill his mark?"

"Yes, sheriff, except I think Aresh might complete the assassination of Sadie and Mr. H himself and not risk having another hitman who has second thoughts."

"Tell me why I shouldn't arrest you right now for attempted murder and throw you in a cell."

"Because you'll be giving me a death sentence. Aresh or his new hitman is on their way to town to kill me, Sadie, and Mr. H. If you put me in a jail cell, I will be a sitting target unable to flee or protect myself. You will be signing my death warrant and allowing a terrorist to win. Sadie and Mr. Habbib will be his next targets, and you have no way to protect them. I am the only person who knows what Aresh looks like and might be able to identify him when he gets to town. He claimed he already bought a ticket. I am your only hope for saving two lives."

The sheriff and Deputy Murphy went into the other room to confer. Distraught, Mark Houtman told Murphy, "I can't lose Sadie. What do we do? We need to stop this madness."

A half-hour later, Sheriff Houtman told Ali, "I am placing you under temporary house arrest for the shooting and attempted assassination of Sadie and Mr. Omar Habbib. However, we have decided because of your confession and your willingness to cooperate in trying to prevent this assassination by another hitman, that we reserve a final judgement. These are the forms for you to fill out to officially apply for sanctuary as a refugee.

"Omar, I am releasing Ali to your custody pending trial or status as a refugee being granted. Your brother, Samuel, is our lawyer who deals with refugees seeking asylum. I will get his advice in the next couple of days, and if he is available, he will contact you and Ali, and we will proceed from there.

"Ali, you are to check in each day with me or Deputy Murphy. Here is my number and Deputy Murphy's. You or Omar can call either of us at any time if you feel threatened or have any problems. If you intend to go with Ahmram to Sports Day at his school, I suggest that Mr. H and Gramps coordinate a protection detail with Mr. Brump. Deputy Murphy and I will be there if we can.

"Meanwhile, we have a terrorist to track down and prevent from harming anyone in our town, and I need to see Sadie and make her aware of the assassination plot," said a harried sheriff.

Ali and Omar left and went home to see Ahmram, contact Mr. Brump, and deal with some extremely complicated paperwork.

Chapter 41

Dilemma–My Life or Hers

Wayne was having second thoughts about continuing his career as a hitman. When he agreed to get rid of Horatio Nelson, it was simply another assignment. Wayne had been developing quite a reputation as a trusted hitman through his 'Speaker's Bureau.' Not only did people find him trustworthy, but now they were willing to pay remarkably high prices for these hits. *Soon I will be able to amass enough money to do anything I want and go wherever sounds good and exciting. That is if I complete these killings.*

It's almost funny how quickly Billy believed my lie about my absences. He's still young and naïve. I hate that I will destroy his innocence, but my father taught me that I needed to do anything it took to survive. I became adept at shoplifting and picking the pockets of rich tourists. When we arrived in Pittman, I went to the local high school. I developed a successful side job as a drug pusher to the teens who were into drugs. I never got caught thanks to my dad's training.

At school, only the band members respected me because of my prowess with the trumpet. Asher and Mike became my only friends. They also supported me when I tried to go legit and open a motorcycle business. I had hoped that I could change, but when I was approached with an offer I couldn't resist, I was hooked.

As a hitman, killing someone was easy for me. The marks selected were just scoundrels who didn't deserve to live. I agreed to kill Nelson because I can't stand cheaters. I felt I was doing a good deed for my community by ridding the town of someone laundering money for a drug cartel. I'm very good at justifying my actions.

All my hits so far have been on evil people, who deserved to die. However, this next hit will be different. I know Sadie and Mr. Habbib, and they don't have an evil bone in their bodies. Should I cross that line and kill innocent, good people?

****

No wonder anxiety is running rampant in Pittman; a killer is on the loose; a store owner has been killed, and an assassin still has not killed all his marks. I need to scrap this video cast whether Andy agrees or not.

On my way to see Lola and Robin, I spotted the sheriff going into Sweet Indulgences. I was curious about how far the sheriff has gotten in his investigation, so I decided to get a chocolate sundae and eavesdrop on any conversations going on at the restaurant. That should seal the deal of whether I should proceed with the video cast or just get out of town as quickly as possible.

Chapter 42

I Must Disappear

Cameron savored his chocolate sundae as he eavesdropped on Sheriff Houtman's conversation with Sadie at Sweet Indulgences, but he didn't like what he was hearing.

The sheriff knew about the second hitman but was unsure who hired him. He has his suspicions, but no concrete evidence. The sheriff warns Sadie that he also knows there is a contract on her life. Again, he says he suspects someone, but he's not sure who the hitman is.

Sadie is now warned, but I know if she is warned, there's a good chance that she will defend herself with the gun she always carries. I need to disappear now.

When the sheriff leaves, Sadie spots Cameron and approaches his table. "How is everything going with the video? Are you and Andy almost finished?"

"We are. We plan to edit it tonight, then I will return to Boston to show my bosses. I'm sure everyone will be pleased."

"When will we be able to see the video? I hope we get a final say on the content."

"You may not be able to see the final video until after we have edited and have it approved by our bosses. It may take a couple of weeks. Until then, I will be in Boston and won't be returning to Pittman until the week before it airs. If you or Robin want any changes, we can make them then. Thank you for all your help, and please thank Lola and Robin for me."

"I feel a little uneasy that we can't see the finished product as soon as you and Andy finish editing. Can't you show us tomorrow before you leave for Boston?" asked Sadie.

"Sorry. That won't be possible. Remember, you all trusted me so why so skeptical now?"

Sadie was taken aback by Cameron's defensive attitude. As soon as he left, she called Robin and Lola and related the gist of the conversation.

"Cameron has been acting weird lately," Lola said. "I'll call Andy and see what's up."

"Sadie, I know you trust Cameron," I said, "but the sheriff and I have been suspicious of him all along. At first, I thought Mark Houtman was just jealous of Cameron, but now I see why he's suspicious. So far, none of us have been able to trace his background before four years ago when he turned up in Boston and became this investigative journalist. I hope we're wrong, but I'm tempted to see if the sheriff can legally seize his video before he leaves tonight."

"That's a fair request considering Cameron's defensive attitude. Call the sheriff now before Cameron disappears."

****

Cameron was back at the hotel packing all his things. He planned to slip out, leaving a note for Andy that the boss had called him back to Boston for an emergency meeting. He would say that he would return in four days. This excuse would buy him time to get an airline ticket with a fake name and a passport so that neither the sheriff, Aresh, or Wayne could trace his whereabouts.

Cameron grabbed all his technical equipment and his suitcases and stopped at the front desk to check out. "I need to leave for Boston," he said to the clerk. "My boss wants me to take the next express bus tonight to reach Boston before tomorrow morning. Thank you for your kindness. Also, will you please see that Andy gets this note?"

"I'll give it to him when he returns to the hotel. Will you need a car to the bus station?"

"No, I have a rental car, and I'll call my photographer to have him pick it up at the bus station tomorrow."

"Why don't you just have your photographer come and take you to the station? It would be more efficient."

"No, I don't want to bother Andy. He might be out on a date, and I don't want to ruin it for him."

"Thank you, Mr. Coldren, we have enjoyed having you here. You've brought quite a bit of excitement to our town." Cameron plunked his room key on the counter and left in such a hurry that he didn't even wait for the receipt to be printed.

****

Wayne decided he just couldn't cross that line by killing people who didn't deserve to die. Sadie is a good person. She supported him when he decided to go into partnership with Billy. She showed faith in him even though he didn't deserve it. Sadie just accepted him for who he was. That's a rare person. He can't betray her trust, and he regrets putting her in danger, but now he faced an unimaginable situation. Mr. Habbib is liked by everyone in Pittman. His son,

Ahmram, loves to come into the motorcycle showroom and climb on the bikes, pretending he is speeding down the highway. Wayne hopes Mr. Habbib and Sadie both survive Aresh's next assassination attempt.

I have to hurry and get out of town fast, and I need to warn Sadie and Mr. Habbib of the danger they are in.

As soon as Wayne made this life-altering decision, he put his escape plan into action.

The first thing he dealt with was his business. He left a transfer document, selling both the motorcycle showroom and the repair shop to Billy for one dollar. He dissolved the partnership with Billy and assigned a huge check to himself for severance pay. He will convert this check into cash as soon as possible. This will provide him with the means to settle anywhere he wishes. He also took several blank checks in case he needed more money wherever he went.

Next, Wayne went home and packed his belongings, ready to leave under the cover of darkness. He drove to the showroom and chose a shiny black Harley to load in the back of his truck. This will provide a speedy form of transportation, wherever he lands.

Last of all, Wayne wrote a note:

Billy,

I am so, so sorry. I got myself into a terrible predicament. I need to leave this country before I am arrested for murder or killed, and no lawyer, not even Mr. Habbib's brother can save me. Please thank Mike and Asher for their friendship over the past several years. Please thank Sadie and Mr. Habbib and tell them to watch their backs because Aresh or his hitman is out to kill them. Tell them they must get protection now. There isn't much time.

Give my enclosed confession to the sheriff. Tell him that I'm sorry. Explain that I was motivated by greed. I never grew up with money and when I saw a chance to earn big money, I betrayed everyone. Make sure that he and Deputy Murphy protect Sadie and Mr. Habbib. I would feel terrible if anything happened to them.

Don't try to contact me. I'll be far gone by the time you read this.

Your stupid friend and ex-partner,

Wayne

Under cover of darkness, Wayne gunned the engine of his truck, loaded with the motorcycle and all of his belongings, and took off for lands unknown to himself and, hopefully, unknown to anyone else. He fingered the fake passport in his pocket and knew he needed to get out of the country before the sheriff disseminated his identity to the border agents and to the airlines, trains, and bus stations. As he approached the border crossing into Canada, he took a deep breath and drove straight ahead with confidence, stopped at the crossing and handed over his passport.

The agent said, "Mr. Bringham, why do you have a motorcycle in the back of your truck?"

"I am delivering it from my boss, Billy Wood, who owns a shop in Pittman. The young man who bought it enjoys racing, and this beauty is a great racer. I'm sure he will be happy riding your many beautiful trails on this motorcycle."

"How long will you be in Canada?"

"About four days. I want to see a bit of your beautiful country before I head back to work."

"Okay, Mr. Bringham, your papers seem to be in order, and your bill of sale from Mr. Wood seems proper. Enjoy your stay in Canada."

"Thank you, sir." Wayne crossed the border, drove a few miles, and stopped under a tree on the side of the road. There he sat on the grass, covered his face with his hands, and cried and cried. He cried for his stupid greed. He cried for poor Nelson, a hateful man, and all of his other terminated marks. *Who am I to choose whether a man should live or die?* He cried for Sadie and Mr. Habbib. "I truly hope they will survive."

Wayne resolved to make a new honest life for himself. Yes, his past with his dad had shaped his life thus far, but now, he resolved to reform, thanks to friends and people who cared for him.

He drove off into the sharp winds of a Canadian night.

Chapter 43

Ski Fest

November dawned bright and sunny with a chill in the air. Everything looked so enticing at the opening of the Ski Fest. I wandered around and saw lines at all the food booths and rides. People were laughing and spending a lot of money. Everyone in town will benefit from their generosity. It was about time we decided to gather again to have fun.

Mr. Brump, Sheriff Houtman, and Deputy Murphy made their presence known so they could keep us all safe.

The only problem that arose was at the motorcycle rides. One of the local teenagers fell off his bike. Billy immediately called the squad, and the EMTs told the parents they were transporting their son to the hospital to be treated for a possible fractured elbow.

Billy was devastated as the frustrated father shouted, "You should be more responsible. I hope you have good insurance." His wife tried to calm him down.

Billy said to Deputy Murphy, "I don't think our insurance will cover accidents off the store's premises. I'm in trouble."

Deputy Murphy said, "Don't worry, Billy. I'll talk to both parents. When the dad calms down, I'm sure I can convince him not to sue you. If talking to the parents doesn't work, I'll get Mr. Samuel Habbib, the lawyer, to help you."

****

The next day, Billy was worrying about a lawsuit when he spotted the note on the table. When he read the note from Wayne, he jumped up, grabbed the checkbook, and checked his store's finances. Billy then called Sheriff Houtman, Sadie, Lola, and Robin. Like a determined posse, they all marched to the jail. Billy stopped at Wayne's place to make sure he was gone. Then he brought up the rear of the group.

Deputy Murphy saw the marchers approaching. "Sheriff, here comes trouble."

Lola led the parade as if she were a majorette in a band. "Sheriff," she yelled as she marched up to the waiting lawmen.

"What is going on?" demanded the bewildered sheriff.

Lola continued, "We're here seeking justice for our town. We've done your job for you once again. We present you with Horatio Nelson's murderer." With a flourish, Lola held out Wayne's written confession. "We also are demanding protection for Sadie, Mr. Habbib, and everyone in our town. This madness must stop. Hitmen, assassins, terrorists, are closing ranks and threatening the very existence of our small town. Mess with our town, and you mess with me and all of my friends."

Everyone started talking at once, and then Sadie yelled, "Stop talking. Stop marching. This isn't Lebanon, but we are being threatened, not by an unknown threat, but by a terrorist leader and his goons. Sheriff, here is a photo of Aresh I found in my family photos. He'll look a little older, but an FBI sketch artist should be able to age the photo. You need to get Aresh's photo out to all law enforcement personnel, the FBI, and the anti-terror task force, and plaster his photo in every airport, port, bus station, train station, and border crossing. You need to tap into every suspected terrorist cell known in this country and tap into the hitman database kept by the FBI and all law enforcement agencies. This is how you can protect us, not by locking us up in a safe house for protection. Do it now."

"Sadie, calm down. I told you all to let the police handle this investigation. I am grateful for your information, but I can't have a bunch of self-appointed vigilantes running around town. Give me the photograph, and I will circulate it and protect our town."

Mr. Brump saw the protestors advancing to the jail and came immediately, listened to the demands, and then stepped forward. "Sheriff, Sadie is experienced in the ways of terrorists, as am I. As a former policeman, I will organize the task force for you. We will have protective coverage for every event, park, festival, church service, or large gathering. When you and Deputy Murphy contact the proper authorities and have them come to Pittman, I'll help them in any way I can. Tell them that I used to coordinate police protection for all events in Chicago following threats from bombers, gangs, and terrorists. I can certainly organize a protection plan for Pittman."

Grateful for Mr. Brump's offer, Sheriff Houtman turned to the marchers. "Let's not waste any time. Go home now, and each of you pair up with someone for protection. Spread the word to your neighbors that we have identified the thief, the sniper at Tanglewood, and Nelson's murderer. Then tell everyone that there is still a threat from an unknown hitman. No one is to go out alone. I'll make copies of the suspected terrorist for you to spread to your neighbors. Report any sightings to Deputy Murphy or Mr. Brump."

Everyone understood what was at stake. They went home to their loved ones, and began the task of spreading the news to the local community.

****

The entire town of Pittman was grateful to hear the sheriff and deputy solved the mysteries of the thefts, the shooting at Tanglewood, and the murder of Nelson. They resolved to protect one another from any other threats and try to quell their community's fears. They then walked to St. Martin's Catholic Church to celebrate the relief they felt and to share their desire for peace.

Halfway through the celebratory Mass, a door opened in the rear of the church, and a masked man with an AK47 burst in and fired several rapid rounds over the congregation's heads, which unfortunately hit the organist and an altar boy. This deranged man then ordered those in the last four rows of the church to march down the aisle and line up in front of the altar.

The deranged shooter then grabbed the microphone out of the priest's hand and shouted out his manifesto against all authority figures and those who are trying to squelch the movement for a new world order. "These authorities are oppressive monsters who seek to steal our very souls."

Still waving his weapon around at the group of

worshippers, the madman spotted Sadie in the congregation and said, "Sadie, you are one of the main monsters. I know you worked with the Resistance in your country against my group in ISIS. We always seek revenge for those who joined the Resistance and for your misguided plots against the saviors of our society.

"I came here to hunt you and Mr. Habbib down and make you pay for your betrayal of my family and your country when you joined the Resistance fighters. Ali was originally sent to perform this deed of revenge, but he is a coward so he will be the first person I execute. Wayne also was hired to kill you, but he too is a coward who can't be trusted. Not only did he refuse to kill you, but he also ran away. Coward! Now, you will watch me kill your friends, then it will be your turn. Make these tyrants lay face down on the floor, now. You know I always follow through with my threats."

The masked shooter ripped off his mask, and everyone gasped at seeing Aresh, a stranger to them all, except to Ali, Sadie, and Omar. Ali hid behind Mr. Brump and whispered to the ex-cop, "That's the leader of my ISIS terrorist group. He will kill me and Sadie and any other person in his way. You've got to stop him. He's insane."

Sadie demurely walked down the aisle with her hands in her pockets and pleaded with the shooter. "Aresh, please don't do this. These people don't deserve this. You're better than this."

Aresh swung his rifle toward the sheriff and yelled, "Sadie, you are a traitor. You love an American! I will now kill your lover and all of his infidel friends while you watch."

When Aresh swung his rifle toward Sheriff

Houtman, Sadie raised her arm toward Aresh. Two shots rang out, and Aresh dropped to the ground, his eyes wide, and his mouth opened in shock.

"You, Mr. Savior, killed my very own brother, a little kid. Who's a coward now?"

The worshippers were stunned by the unexpected turn of events.

"But, sheriff. We heard two shots," I said. "Did Aresh fire at Sadie before she shot him?"

Before the sheriff could respond, Mr. Brump stepped up. "Sadie, I shot Aresh. I didn't want you to have to live with the guilt of killing a fellow countryman. Sheriff, if you look in the wall behind where Aresh was standing, you will see Sadie's bullet. Mine went straight to the madman's heart."

Sheriff Houtman and Deputy Murphy swung into action, confiscating the terrorist's rifle and then checking Aresh's pulse.

Lola and I rushed to Sadie and embraced her. Sadie turned to us with tears streaming down her face. "I'm okay," she said, "I always protect my family, even if I miss my target. Thank you, Mr. Brump."

Attitudes changed in the town that day. Grateful to Sadie and Mr. Brump, the debate was over. Tolerance and respect for other's opinions became the spirit of Pittman, and a new sign went up at the entrance to the town that future generations would puzzle about the origin of for years.

PITTMAN -ALL ARE WELCOME HERE!
WELCOME TO OUR FAMILY!

Chapter 44

Looking to the Future

After things settled down, with Milo and Asher cleared of all charges, Ali awaiting refugee status, and Wayne and Cameron fleeing and disappearing, everyone took the time to breathe and join together in the Pittman Forest for a celebratory community potluck.

Large tables were set with mouth-watering plates of all types of food from casseroles, to regional and ethnic specialties, and, of course, a dessert table. Bart O'Neal, our famous grill chef, fried hamburgers, ribs, veggie burgers, hot dogs, chicken, and brats. Some of the community members came early and set up tables and chairs in large and small groupings.

Mike, Billy, and Asher also came early and huddled together to finalize their plans for after graduation hoping to announce those plans to a supportive audience.

Omar Habbib, his brother, Samuel, and Ali were engrossed in conversation as Ahmram looked on.

Lola, Marie, and Mr. Brump were in charge of entertainment, and as usual, Edna Mae was emcee. Sadie and I sat together watching our scattered children, adopted children, and friends. I said to Sadie, "Well, that's over, mysteries solved. I wonder what is next?"

"I hope only for a season of tranquility," Sadie

said. "I'm looking forward to a winter season where we have time to cuddle up by our fireplaces, and just watch the snow swirl and fall. That's what I enjoy most about my new home, other than the people, of course." We looked up when Edna Mae resumed her role as emcee.

"Ladies and gentlemen," Edna Mae began, "step right up to the serving tables and fill your plates. Save the dessert table for a little later. Take your seats and enjoy our opening performance by our school band and their director."

After we were all seated and while digging joyously into the plethora of goodies, the band played a medley of songs, then Marie stepped up to the microphone and once more charmed us all with a beautiful aria from "Carmen."

After that, Lola was introduced as Madame Rosa, a famous seer. Our gifted actress produced a small table and with a flourish, placed a tablecloth decorated with stars on the table. She threw a cape similarly decorated over her shoulders. Placing a crystal ball in the center of the table, she donned an elegant headscarf and intoned, "MMMM, MMMM, Oh Great Swami, share with us our futures."

As laughter filled the park, Edna Mae announced, "Our first guests will be three lovable young men, Mike, Asher, and Billy."

"Madame Rosa, we want to tell all our plans for the future," said Mike.

"Proceed, my sons," said Swami Rosa.

Asher looked straight at me and said, "I have decided to apply for early admission in December to MIT. My backup schools during the spring admission period will be Dartmouth, Boston College, and

Princeton. I hope to pursue a career in finance and math. I'm sorry, Mom, but I don't want to return to Kentucky for college. I need to stay near enough to visit you and my friends."

He bowed, and Mike stepped up to the microphone. "Oh, Swami Lola, I mean Rosa, I also have plans but more business-oriented. I am headed to Florida and opening a surf shop within a bowling alley. I have a friend I met at school who is from Florida. He is moving back to Pompano Beach and wants to partner with me in this venture. I'm sure with my experience running my dad's bowling alley, and my friend's experience with the whole world of surfing, we can make it a success."

Swami Rosa led a round of applause and then introduced our beloved Billy, who had been overwhelmed with all the work since Wayne disappeared. Swami Rosa also called on Deputy Robert Murphy to join Billy at the microphone. Murphy blushed as he handed Swami Rosa a bouquet.

Billy faced the microphone and said, "As you all know, it is difficult running a motorcycle showroom and a repair shop. I had planned to combine shops and rent out the other one. However, Robert Murphy proposed an offer I can't refuse. Robert will become my new partner. He plans to leave law enforcement and run the showroom. He will be a natural salesman since he knows all of you in our community. I will continue to work in the repair shop and have time to attend a business school in Albany part-time. This will allow me to learn about accounts, billing, and advertising."

The boys and Robert Murphy all bowed and got a standing ovation from the crowd.

Edna Mae said, "Everyone, take a break now to discuss these developments. Step up to the dessert table and see Mr. Brump for ice cream cones. He is scooping two flavors, chocolate, and chocolate chip. Wander around, enjoy the fresh air, and meet back here in thirty minutes for other major announcements. Don't leave yet, or you will have to get second-hand gossip instead of the real thing."

Chapter 45

As the Sun Sets

When Edna Mae called everyone back together, she announced, "Sheriff Houtman has something to say."

"I just want to extend a heartfelt thank you to Sadie, Robin, and the Super Sleuths. I know I've been an absolute pain when it comes to listening to your suggestions, but I couldn't have solved these mysteries without you. I often jumped to conclusions too early and failed to examine all the facts. For this, I am truly sorry and grateful that you refused to let me fail.

"Also, if there are any journalists here, and if any of you in the audience are taking pictures, I plead with you not to post any information or pictures of Sadie or Mr. Habbib. We don't want any other vengeful terrorists tracking them down.

"I am going to miss your partnership, Robert. I'm sure you will make a wonderful salesman. I might even be convinced to buy a motorcycle. I wish to thank you, Robert, for being a wonderful partner and my friend. I'm not sure what I will do without you. Robert and I will be interviewing candidates to replace him, and I also will be hiring Mr. Brump as a part-time investigator. Without his help, we couldn't have solved these crimes because we would have been too exhausted to think. Thank you all. Let's keep Pittman the close community it is and refuse to welcome any criminals."

I saw many of those in the audience nodding their heads and crying. I'm sure Deputy Murphy will be missed greatly as our lawman. He is loved by all.

With a drum roll by the percussion section of the band, Lola, without her cape, and dressed in a flowery cotton dress, went up to the front, pulling Andy behind her. "Sadly, but happily, I will be leaving Pittman for the winter season and moving to New York. My director of *The Taming of the Shrew*, where I have been portraying Kate at Shakespeare and Company, has asked me to audition next week for a part in his new adaptation of an Agatha Christie play that he will be directing off-Broadway. I will be the first ever female inspector in an Agatha Christie mystery. In partnership with Ms. Marple, I can invent so many new ways to portray the Inspector. My director friend assures me that I am perfect for the part. If I get the part, I will be leaving very soon. I've already found an apartment to rent."

Andy came next. "I also will be moving to New York. A popular travel magazine, *Travel and Leisure,* has offered me the job of head photographer for the travel section of the magazine. For this job, I will be able to travel the world—at their expense—following the authors of the articles to many tourist spots and exotic venues all over the USA. Since I will only be in my apartment in New York sporadically, I have agreed to share an apartment with Lola. The price of apartments in Manhattan and Brooklyn are sky-high, so this will benefit each of us. Thank you all for being so welcoming to me.

Lola and Andy bowed, holding hands, and raising them in a victory pose. We all stood and cheered through our tears. I whispered to Sadie, "I can't believe I will be losing both Lola and Asher. I don't think I'm looking forward to letting my baby birds fly away."

While we were all looking at each other in amazement, Omar Habbib and Ali stepped up.

Omar said, "I will be taking over Ten Pins Bowling Alley until Mike's dad is released from prison. Welcome, one and all. If you are a local Pittman resident, you will be entitled to one free game of bowling or one free snack from our new menu at the bar in Ten Pins. See you there at our grand reopening in January.

"As you know, Ali has been living with me for many months. We have appreciated every moment he spent in our home, and we wish him well in his next venture. Milo will now live in our home, and I am sure that he and Ahmram will be good friends."

Ahmram stood up and cheered, then ran to Ali and gave him a big hug before throwing a kiss to Milo in the audience.

Ali said, "Ladies and gentlemen of the Berkshires, I owe you all a big thank you. Thank you to Sheriff Houtman for not arresting me after I shot the rifle at Tanglewood and scared you all. He understood the circumstances of the attempted shooting and understood why I deliberately missed. When I offered to help him track down Aresh, the terrorist leader, in order to prevent future attempts at killing, he offered me a deal that included house incarceration and assistance in his further arrests. In exchange, he offered me a pardon for my crime. Thank you all from the bottom of my heart.

"Now that the killer is dead and all other suspects are dealt with one way or another, I have the sheriff's permission to move on. I too am going to Brooklyn, New York, where a friend of Omar Habbib owns a butcher shop. I am going to be the owner's apprentice, and if Omar ever realizes his dream of opening his own butcher shop just like his father had in Lebanon, I, a new refugee to the USA, will return to Pittman to work with him." Ali turned to Ahmram, hugged him, and said, "Ahmram, this means I will be back. I'm only going to be away for a little while."

Ahmram said to all in the community, "I love it here in America and love our Pittman family." He then held his hands in the air and yelled, "YES."

Everyone in the audience was crying by this point. They felt relief that the mysteries were solved, and their fear was over, but they came to the realization that major change was in the

wind.

****

I woke with a start, unsure whether I had slept six hours or ten. I looked toward the window and stared at a blazing red sun rising in the east. Stunned by its beauty, I sighed and hoped it didn't signal a warning as it did to sailors. I needed a future filled with hope and happiness for myself and all my friends and family.

My thoughts turned to Matt and the possibilities ahead for us.

Change is in the air, and I'm looking forward to it. I'll have an empty nest soon enough. Right now, I want to fill that nest with an abundance of possibilities.

Sadie's Lebanese Recipe, adapted for Working Parents

Though in Lebanon, everyone follows traditional recipes, Sadie has discovered, as a working woman, she doesn't have time for the traditional time-consuming recipes she learned from her mother. She has modernized them, and surprisingly, they taste just as good, if not better.

Modernized Lebanese Kousa

Recipe Ingredients:

One 8 or 16 oz. can tomato juice
Zucchini - Your choice of number and size
Filling:
½ pound of ground lamb
1 or ½ cup long grain, white rice
1 Tablespoon of tomato paste, less if using ½ cup rice
About a ½ teaspoon of salt
About ½ teaspoon of pepper
A generous sprinkle of cinnamon

Preparation:

—Brown the lamb in a nonstick skillet.
—Put browned lamb in a bowl, add rice, tomato paste, and seasonings then mix.
—Cut zucchinis in half lengthwise.
—With a spoon, scoop out the center of the zucchinis, leaving an indentation to fill.
—Fill the zucchini halves with a generous scoop of the filling.
Place zucchinis in a baking pan.

Cover the Kousa with tomato juice and a sprinkle of cinnamon.
Cover the baking pan with foil.
Bake at 350 degrees until the rice is cooked.

Lebanese recipes use the taste test for seasonings. These recipes have been passed down in the families from generation to generation, so the numbers given are approximations. Try out the taste test.

A word about the author...

Ms. Jacobs is a writer, a teacher of Creative Writing, and a writing coach. She has published essays and poems in various publications. She is thrilled with the responses from readers of her first book, *Don't Mess with Me* in the Berkshire Mystery Series, and hopes her readers will enjoy this second book in the series, *Peril in Pittman*, Book Two in the Berkshire Mystery Series.

You can contact Ms. Jacobs at maryannjacobsauthor@gmail.com

Website: https://maryannjacobsauthor.wordpress.com/

Thank you for purchasing
this publication of The Wild Rose Press, Inc.

For questions or more information
contact us at
info@thewildrosepress.com.

The Wild Rose Press, Inc.
www.thewildrosepress.com